"Look at the stars with me, Jasmine," Matt commanded, slipping his arm around her shoulders.

For a moment Jasmine was more aware of his closeness, his hard muscles pressing against her softness, than of the myriad of shimmering lights in the dark sky above them. She tilted her head back, feeling the delicate hairs on her nape brush his sweater, and shivered with sensual pleasure.

"There's a falling star," he said softly, his breath caressing her cheek. "We used to wish on them when we were kids."

"Did you wish just then?" she asked.

"Yes." His voice was a deep rumble.

"What did you wish?"

"I wished," he murmured, "for you to turn around and kiss me."

"Well, I wouldn't want to keep a wish from coming true," she said, her pulse skipping.

He tightened his arms around her. Lowering his lips to hers, he made his wish again, and suddenly the sky was filled with a thousand falling stars. . . .

WHAT ARE *LOVESWEPT* ROMANCES?

They are stories of true romance and touching emotion. We
believe those two very important ingredients are constants
in our highly sensual and very believable stories in the
LOVESWEPT line. Our goal is to give you, the reader,
stories of consistently high quality that may sometimes make
you laugh, sometimes make you cry, but are always fresh
and creative and contain many delightful surprises within
their pages.

Most romance fans read an enormous number of books.
Those they truly love, they keep. Others may be traded with
friends and soon forgotten. We hope that each *LOVESWEPT*
romance will be a treasure—a "keeper." We will always try
to publish

LOVE STORIES YOU'LL NEVER FORGET
BY AUTHORS YOU'LL ALWAYS REMEMBER

The Editors

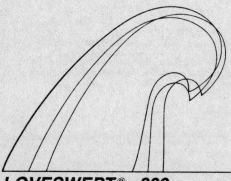

LOVESWEPT® • 209

Sara Orwig
Visions of Jasmine

BANTAM BOOKS
TORONTO • NEW YORK • LONDON • SYDNEY • AUCKLAND

VISIONS OF JASMINE

A Bantam Book / September 1987

*LOVESWEPT® and the wave device are registered
trademarks of Bantam Books, Inc. Registered in U.S. Patent
and Trademark Office and elsewhere.*

*If you would be interested in receiving protective vinyl
covers for your Loveswept books, please write to this address
for information:*

> *Loveswept*
> *Bantam Books*
> *P.O. Box 985*
> *Hicksville, NY 11802*

ISBN 0-553-21833-6

Published simultaneously in the United States and Canada

---

*Bantam Books are published by Bantam Books, Inc. Its trade-
mark, consisting of the words "Bantam Books" and the por-
trayal of a rooster, is registered in U.S. Patent and Trademark
Office and in other countries. Marca Registrada. Bantam
Books, Inc., 666 Fifth Avenue, New York, New York 10103.*

PRINTED IN THE UNITED STATES OF AMERICA

O   0 9 8 7 6 5 4 3 2 1

With love to David

One

Off the coast of Argentina, out of sight of the eastern shoreline of Patagonia, a trawler bobbed in the ocean, while its passengers scurried about frantically. Flames danced around the *Pelican*'s engine compartment hatch, the burning wood crackling and popping. Shouts mingled with the roar of the fire and the splash of rubber life rafts hitting the water. Jasmine Kirby coughed and blinked as she passed a stack of notebooks to the next person in line.

"Keep the records moving!" Gary Hobart called. His brown hair was tousled, his brow damp with perspiration, as he received a handful of papers. The ship bobbed in the dark water, flames licking eagerly at the old wood.

"Come on, rain!" he snapped, glancing skyward and listening to the rumble of thunder. "Everyone keep calm. We have time to save our records."

"What about the gasoline?" Jasmine asked, thinking about the extra supply of fuel they carried on board because they had been working in an isolated area.

"The fire isn't that far along yet," Gary answered grimly.

Without replying, she worked furiously, passing the records the wildlife group had made down the line. Her braid of black hair swung against her back as she twisted and turned. Her long legs, clad in jeans, were spread apart to brace her body as she accepted a stack of papers from Tim O'Rourke. In turn, she handed them quickly to Ginny Knight.

Suddenly, Gary called a halt to the work. "We have to get off now! Everyone off. Come on, Jasmine." He took her arm. "Look, you go in the dinghy with the records. I'll be with you in a second."

"Sure," she said as he helped her over the side. For a moment she paused to look into his velvety black eyes.

"You've done a great job," Gary said, wiping his brow. "Into the boat now."

As she glanced beyond him, she saw the flames shoot higher, consuming more of the old trawler that had been donated to the Green Earth wildlife group, and she realized Gary had waited until the last possible second to abandon ship in order to save as many of the records as possible.

She climbed down into the wooden dinghy. It was filled with ledgers, pictures, and papers, all enclosed in plastic bags. Gary flung a tarp down on top of the records, and she spread it over them. She waited expectantly as the last members of the science team climbed into the other two life rafts, and Gary descended the rope ladder.

As Gary swung his foot out over the dinghy to step down and join her, a blast shook the *Pelican*, rocking the little dinghy dangerously. Water splashed, washing Gary off the ladder. He fell into the icy water, but Tim was able to haul him quickly on board one of the life rafts.

"Row!" Gary yelled. "Before the *Pelican* blows and sinks us all!"

Frightened that the trawler would explode, Jasmine pulled hard on the oars, momentarily unconcerned that she was alone in her boat.

Currents and the wind were causing an ever-widening rift between Jasmine's dinghy and the two life rafts, but all three were still in sight of each other. Then the flames hit the extra fuel and chemicals, and the *Pelican* exploded with a loud boom, a flash of fire, and a billow of black smoke.

As bits and pieces of the trawler flew through the air, Jasmine dropped down and covered her head.

After several seconds she sat up. The night was gray with storm clouds; the water was inky against the lighter sky. All that was left of the *Pelican* was debris.

"Jasmine, row this way!" Gary called.

"I am," she cried, as she tried desperately to row the boat. She could hear the others calling back and forth, but within minutes fear was welling up inside her. The wind had risen, and she had to fight the force of it as the first drops of rain fell.

"Jasmine!"

"Over here!"

"We're coming. Keep rowing!" Gary called, while she struggled with all her might to go faster toward the sound of his voice. Then a sweeping curtain of cold, stinging rain poured down on her, and she pulled out the tarp to wrap it protectively around herself.

When the rain had lessened to a gentle patter, she flung the tarp aside and called, "Gary! Gary!"

There was no answer, only a rumble of thunder, and she felt a stabbing jolt of panic. She pulled the tarp back over her head. "Keep calm," she mumbled to herself. "Just keep calm. Gary said someone would look for us tomorrow and when they do, they'll look for all of us no matter how spread apart we are." It sounded logical, and she calmed her nerves, continuing to talk to herself. "I have enough provisions. I'm in a boat and I'm safe. I was able to save my passport and some money. The worst of the storm is over. The others aren't far away. The wind is dying."

The storm had blown her ahead of the others, she reasoned. If she rowed in the opposite direction now, before she started drifting, she might get back to them. Ignoring the steady mist, she rowed until the realization struck her that she might be going in circles.

"Idiot! Why don't you use your brain, Jasmine!" she said, as she reached for the flare gun. Aiming the gun overhead, she fired, hoping that Gary or someone in the other raft would send an answering signal.

The flare burst overhead, red, radiant, reassuring. She waited expectantly, then nervously, and finally faced the disappointing fact that they hadn't seen it.

How could they miss the flare? she wondered in dismay. It should be visible for miles. As swiftly as the question came she had her answer, as another cloudburst poured rain for several minutes. She pulled the protective tarp over the dinghy and her head. If the others had been huddled beneath a tarp, they wouldn't have seen her flare, she thought.

When the rain stopped, she tried another flare. After waiting in vain for a response she settled into the boat to sleep, pulling the tarp over her again for warmth.

She opened her eyes, momentarily thinking she was on the *Pelican*, then memory returned and she sat up. The sun was above the horizon, its rays spreading glistening silver streamers across the smooth blue water. The air was fresh after the rain, and the sea was calm—and empty!

"Don't panic, Jasmine Kirby," she said sternly to herself. "Today you'll be rescued. You'll be with the others. This little episode will be an amusing adventure to laugh at over dinner tonight."

She fished out one of the emergency food packs, and peeled open some orange juice. Then she opened a packet of dehydrated apple slices. While the dinghy drifted, she nibbled on the apples and drank the juice, feeling thankful she had skin that could take the sun. She had tanned a golden brown from working on board the *Pelican* and outdoors on Tierra del Fuego with the science group.

The day was as endless as the ocean. Once a pink jellyfish floated by just below the water's surface, and as much as she disliked jellyfish, she leaned on the edge of the dinghy to talk to it.

By midafternoon she was having difficulty keeping calm. She ate more of the stored food and decided she had better think about saving herself instead of waiting for help to come. She determined the compass directions from the position of the sun and then she rowed. Land had to be to the west.

About an hour later she spotted a dot on the horizon to the north. Her pulse jumped, and she carefully stood up to peer at the speck, then sat down and took the oars again. Her spirits soared. She could finally make out a sail!

"A boat!" She envisioned a big sailing ship with a crew like the *Love Boat*'s. There would be a great flurry of activity as they contacted her friends who no doubt had been rescued by now. With renewed energy she rowed wildly, filled with joy as the sails loomed larger, and the gap between the dinghy and the ship narrowed.

"People! A hot shower, food, water . . . chocolate milk!" she shouted excitedly. She pictured a handsome captain in a sparkling white uniform. He would lift her on board and one of the women passengers would lend her a dress and they would all dine together that night as they sailed toward the nearest port.

For a moment she stared down at her red sweater and the silly plastic penguin pinned to it. She had bought the pin as a souvenir in Ushuaia. Then she drifted back into her fantasy world, watching happily as the white sail began to look much bigger to her. The hull was brown, and the name, *Paradise*, was painted on the bow. *Paradise!* It was the most beautiful sight she had ever seen.

"Yoo-hoo! Hey!" she screamed, waving her hands

wildly. "Hey! Help! *Socorro! Ayudame por favor!*" Excitement blurred everything. There was a boat—a haven, rescue! That was all she could think of or see as the dinghy bumped gently against the side. The *Love Boat!* Where was the captain and the smiling crew?

"Hey! Help! I need help! *Ayudame! Buenas tardes!*"

Matthew Forsythe Rome opened his eyes and blinked. He yawned and stretched.

"Help!"

He blinked again. It hadn't been a dream. He had heard someone yelling for help.

"What in the blue blazes?" he mumbled, sitting up and peering at an empty expanse of sea.

"Ayudame, por favor."

Leaning over the side of the ship, he looked in the direction of the voice that was persistently calling for help. He wondered if he were still dreaming. A solitary woman—with curves in all the right places—was in a dinghy filled with papers and books. He stared openmouthed, thinking that he shouldn't have taken a nap in the bright sunshine.

Jasmine's pulse jumped when his head appeared over the side. "I'm lost!"

"Wait a minute." The head disappeared, and she smiled. She was rescued! And he spoke English. She imagined the rest of the crew and the captain would appear to welcome her now. In seconds both a painter and a rope ladder tumbled down over the side. Securing the dinghy to the former, she scrambled up the latter swiftly and climbed aboard with the man's help. Once on the deck, she looked at a bare chest that made her temporarily forget her dilemma and her surroundings.

Skin as bronzed as teak, matted with golden chest hair, covered breathtaking pectoral muscles and deltoids.

"You're lost?" a deep voice asked in a slow, lazy drawl. It brought her out of her daze.

"Yes. My ship caught fire and blew up last night and you're the first . . ." Her words faded and her mouth hung open. Her fantasies were crushed like crackers beneath a steam roller. She looked up at him, taking in a rugged face with sharp angles, a crooked beak of a nose, a jaw covered in golden stubble, a tangle of golden hair and a battered sailor cap that looked as if it had been issued during the First World War. Where she had imagined a sparkling white uniform there were amazingly brief, tattered, frayed, *indecent* cutoffs that fit like skin, bare legs, and aging deck shoes. Scars laced his skin, thin white lines that told of a tough life.

She snapped her mouth shut, remembering that however scruffy he was, the man meant safety, rescue, and return to her friends. She smiled.

He smiled in return. It was like looking into the sun. His smile was dazzling and gave him surprising appeal. "Want to look again in case you missed something?" he asked in his lazy drawl.

Oh, lordy. This might not be as easy as she had imagined. "I'm Jasmine Kirby. And I'm lost. From the *Pelican*," she added hastily.

His blue eyes twinkled in a not very reassuring manner. "Howdy. I'm Matthew Rome. So glad to meet you." He offered her his hand. Three minutes ago she would have grabbed it eagerly, but now she was beginning to feel wary. His smile broadened as he waited, and she sighed, accepting his handshake, her hand enclosed in warm, strong fingers that were as noticeable and disturbing as the rest of him.

"How do you do, Mr. Rome."

He leaned over the side. "You alone?"

"Yes, as a matter of fact," she said coolly, unable to resist a glance at his well-muscled legs.

"What's in the boat?"

"Papers. May I bring them on board?" She looked around and this time shock buffeted her. The deck was littered; laundry flapped in the breeze; the wooden hull was chipped and in need of cleaning and repair. She held the line and stared in dismay.

"How long since you last ate?"

"Several hours ago," she mumbled, resisting the temptation to ask him how long since he had last cleaned up around the ship. "Are you alone?"

"Yes, ma'am." He tilted his head to one side. "Your accent sounds familiar. Are you from my home state of Texas?"

"Yes. May I bring my papers on board now and radio the authorities of my whereabouts?"

His smile was as lazy and slow as his drawl. "A fellow Texan," he said with satisfaction. "Yes and yes. I'll get your papers, and I'll radio the mainland, but let's do it in just a minute. You look as if you need to sit down. I'll secure the dinghy and we'll get the papers after you've had a chance to catch your breath."

"I've caught my breath. Where are you headed?"

"Wherever the wind blows," he answered cheerfully. His eyes narrowed. "You travel with a lot of papers. Are you a writer, a lawyer, or a teacher?"

"I'm none of those. The papers are scientific

data accumulated by Green Earth, a team of scientists on a grant to study endangered species of Patagonia."

"You're a zoologist," he said.

"No. I'm a secretary and an efficient one," she replied, wishing he could say the same about sailing.

"So they set you adrift all alone with the papers when the ship blew up?"

"No, they didn't mean to," she said stiffly. "Gary was going to come with me and the—never mind! Let's get the papers on board. They represent two months of work."

"Jasmine," he said, drawing out the name and sending an unwanted tingle radiating through her. "The papers will be okay. There are no storm clouds in sight: the sea is calm. You need to relax and take it easy if you've been adrift alone since last night. Come on, now. You sit down." He looked around, kicked a stack of pots off a barrel, and guided her to it.

She sat down and closed her eyes, wishing Matthew Rome would vanish and the *Love Boat*'s captain would appear in his place.

When she opened her eyes, she realized she had gotten half her wish. Matthew Rome was nowhere in sight. Then she remembered he had gone over the side to secure the dinghy. She looked around again, and her spirits sank a notch. "Why me?" she asked.

"What's that, Jasmine?"

She forced a smile. "Are the records safe and secure?" she asked as he climbed on board. Her gaze was drawn to him as the sunshine made a golden halo of his hair beneath the tattered gray hat. She took in every detail of him, down to the thread that dangled over his ear.

"Sure enough. Now, you come sit over here in the shade of the cockpit where it's cooler, and I'll get you a drink to soothe your ruffled nerves."

"I don't—" She started to tell him she didn't drink, but as she walked toward the cockpit stepping over coiled lines, discarded clothing and sneakers, laundry, and tools, she decided this was the moment in her life to start.

"I guess I will."

"I thought you would," he said, and she glanced at him sharply. He smiled, his eyes twinkled, and she had a feeling he was laughing at her.

With a sweep of his hand he shoved books off a folding chair that had seen better days. It was canted at an odd angle, but when she sat down, the chair didn't collapse as she expected. "I'll be back before you can say Jack Robinson!"

She was sure he would be. She nodded and closed her eyes. Dreams were never like reality. Never, she chided herself. She shouldn't have envisioned the *Love Boat*, and she should be grateful to the bottom of her soul for Matthew Rome. She smiled, opened her eyes, and decided to try to show the man some gratitude.

She wasn't ready to find bare legs at eye level right beside her, with bare, muscular, impressive thighs. She blinked and looked up, trying to skip over the cutoffs and bare chest, but it wasn't easy. He handed her a glass filled with a pale liquid.

"Chilled white wine."

"Thank you," she said, thinking he didn't look like the white wine type. After a few minutes of silence, she asked him, "What do you do, Mr. Rome, when—"

"Excuse me, but call me Matt. After all—we're in a close, intimate situation. Why shouldn't we be on a first-name basis?"

She sat up straighter. "Mr. Rome. I appreciate your rescuing me, but don't get ideas!"

He paused with his drink halfway to his mouth and looked at her with wide eyes. "What kind of ideas?" he asked with great innocence.

She blushed, wondering when a man had made her react that way last. It was doubly annoying to have it happen for the first time in years around a man like Matthew Rome! "You looked as if you were leering," she said bluntly.

He stared at her solemnly and raised his glass in a toast. "Here's to a pleasant rescue. I wasn't leering."

She touched her glass briefly against his and sipped, aware that he was watching her. "You know, Jasmine, you've just been rescued from floating alone in the Atlantic Ocean, but you don't seem too happy about it."

"I'm sorry," she said quickly. "I *am* grateful to you."

"Something aboard my ship has distressed you."

She was nervous. The man didn't seem the type to notice if a whale flopped up on deck, but he did notice tiny details and subtle reactions. "Well," she smiled at him, "while I was adrift I was fantasizing. Foolishness, I know. I imagined being rescued by the crew of the *Love Boat*. Instead . . ." She looked around. "Pardon me, but instead of the *Love Boat* and its captain—I have the *African Queen* and Charlie Allnutt."

He smiled. "Allnutt was a helpful person. At any rate, you're safe," he added briskly. "I'll radio a message, then I'll take you ashore. To whom do I place the call?"

He amazed her. *To whom.* "I'm not sure of any place to call. The *Pelican* was our base of operations, except for tents in the field."

"Do you have any idea what the *Pelican*'s whereabouts were when she blew up?"

She shook her head. "We had started the trek back up the coast. At Buenos Aires I was to leave the team, because my job would be done, and I planned to fly home from there. We were at Río Gallegos on the last stop. Can you tell me how far it is to the nearest port?"

"I'll have to look at the charts. Would you like to freshen up first?"

"Yes, thank you."

He led the way down the companionway. Below deck it was dank and dark. "I didn't expect company," he said cheerfully. "You can have the forward cabin. I usually sleep in the cockpit anyway."

She could see why. She expected a rat to run across her feet at any moment. "Are there any rodents on board?"

He stopped and turned around. "Rodents? Rabbits, squirrels, or mice?"

"Rats! I've heard ships sometimes have rats!"

He pursed his lips. "I can't recall seeing a single one in months."

His answer didn't reassure her, and she glared at his bare back, realizing that his back was one of his better points. It was attractive, tanned, muscled, and too appealing. His whole body was one of his better points. And so far, his ship was his worst. She looked at a long scar that ran from his shoulder blade to his waist with several smaller scars crisscrossing it. He also had a scar on the back of his neck and one on his arm. She wondered what had caused them.

When he opened the door, she gazed at a cabin filled with junk.

"On second thought," he said, "after you freshen up, you might prefer to sleep with me on—"

"I knew it! You *were* leering and you're lecherous and I'm not sleeping with you! I wasn't with you one whole hour before you asked! Of all the people in the world to come to my rescue, I'm stuck with a lecherous, slovenly . . ." Suddenly she was at a loss, and beneath his amused, blue-eyed gaze her words sputtered like firecrackers in the rain.

"Slovenly what?" he asked as if it were the most important bit of information he could hope to hear.

"Sailor!"

"Come on, Jasmine Kirby," he said teasingly. "You can do better than 'sailor.' "

She snapped her mouth shut and went past him into the cabin. "I'll freshen up. Alone!"

He grinned and held his drink up in a salute. "See you above. Oh, let me give you a clean towel." Before she could protest, he passed her, and she caught a surprisingly pleasant scent. As he rummaged through a pile of clothing, she wanted to gnash her teeth.

"Any towel will do," she said in certainty that there was no such thing as a clean towel on board.

"I have a clean one in here. I remember it. It's

orange. Here it is!" He held it up triumphantly and extended it to her.

"Thanks." She snatched it out of his hand.

"Anything else you might need?"

"No, thank you, Mr. Rome."

"Matt. See you above," he said, closing the door behind him. She walked to a port to stare outside in the foolish hope that she would see land. She didn't see anything because the glass was covered with specks on the outside and mildew on the inside.

She tried to avoid stepping on clothing and tools and books, but finally gave up, walking over them as if they didn't exist. She stared at the shower and was stunned to find it was clean. With a sigh of relief, she began to undress.

Half an hour later she went above and found him in the cockpit stretched out in a hammock, a cold beer beside him, his cap covering his face. Nothing had changed since she had gone below and she stared at him in consternation. She had expected he would tidy up, fix something to eat, unload the dinghy, or do something worthwhile. Instead, he had gone to sleep.

And as she stared at him, his face hidden from view, it was impossible to keep from letting her gaze move slowly over his long body. His broad shoulders were impressive, his narrow waist equally so, and he had the muscles of a gymnast. But muscle and bone and body shouldn't have been so provocative when the personality of the man they composed was slightly grating. What was it about him that disturbed her so?

"Look to your heart's content. You can touch too," he said softly from beneath the hat.

She jumped, then stared at him. He had the battered sailor's cap over his face, so how did he know what she was doing? Embarrassed, angered, and dismayed, she leaned closer and saw a tattered hole in the frayed seam and a blue eye looking back at her.

"Want to try my hammock?" he asked in a deep voice.

"No!" Grimacing, she went below to the galley while a deep chuckle seemed to drift down the hatchway behind her.

Two

It was too early for dinner, but she was famished and wanted something hot. Again she found the same startling contrast. The functional part of the galley was as clean as she could hope to find. Supplies were neatly tucked away, the appliances glistened, and her feelings toward Matthew Rome were slightly mollified.

She searched through cabinets and began to hum as she decided on grilled cheese sandwiches. To her delight, she found chocolate powder and powdered milk. She tried to ignore the table covered with pans and shells and kitchen utensils. Some had fallen to the floor and she shoved them aside with her toe until she could walk around without stumbling. Finally she carried the meal to the cockpit.

The wind had come up slightly, and the boat heeled to the starboard side, so Jasmine had to balance as she walked. She paused to look at the sea. Tiny whitecaps curled on the water as the wind played across it, ruffling its surface with invisible touches. The sail caught the breeze, giving a little more motion to the ship. As far as she could see in any direction, there was an unbroken line of blue water that became one with the horizon. The expanse of ocean and the security of the *Paradise* gave her a satisfying feeling that lasted until she looked at the disturbing body stretched beside her. The cap still covered his face and she wasn't about to bend down and see if he had been watching her. But in spite of her intentions, her gaze flicked swiftly over the length of him, and she had to admit the view was impressive.

"Mr. Rome," she said, as she sat on a deck chair near his hammock and placed his dish on the deck.

He lowered the hat and sat up, swinging his feet over the side to sit facing her, their knees almost touching.

"I brought you something to eat," she said.

His eyes twinkled when he smiled. "How nice."

"I couldn't wait for dinner. I'm starved. I hope you like this. Since you stocked the boat, I presume you like cheese sandwiches."

"Mmm," he mumbled as he munched on a bite of the sandwich. "That's good. I was getting tired of my own cooking."

"Did you contact anyone about me?"

"Sure did. I radioed Bahía Grande, which is the closest port, and they will radio back when they learn something about the *Pelican*."

"Thank you. I don't speak Spanish except for a few phrases."

"I can get you to Bahía Grande by noon tomorrow," he said, studying her intently. His glance sent a flutter across her nerves. "Or I can take you north on my cutter to Texas. It's a nice trip."

She smiled. "Thank you, but I'd like to join my friends. If you'll just get me to Bahía Grande, please, I would appreciate it very much."

"Sure. Whatever the lady wants." Matt noticed she had replaited her hair. It glistened darkly in the sunlight, and he gazed at her contentedly. She was lovely. Her features were symmetrical, and her eyes an unusual shade of green, like sea water. Her lips were curved, full, and sensual. She seemed oblivious to his appraisal, and between bites, she picked up a shirt and folded it.

"As soon as we've finished eating, we can unload the dinghy. Those records might be wet. I was in a rainstorm last night right after the *Pelican* blew up." While she talked, she began to pick up some books from the deck and stack them. As she turned back to take a drink, she looked directly into Matt's eyes, and he liked the sensation it caused inside him. She was an appealing, sexy woman.

"Are you married?" he asked her.

"No. I was married once when I was very young, but I'm divorced now." She took a bite of sandwich and chewed, placing another book on the pile, while he wondered what could have caused her divorce.

He tilted his head and studied her a moment longer, thinking what a waste of her beauty it would be, if her chief interest was neatness. He leaned closer to ask, "Are you going to try to tidy up my life?"

She gave him a startled look. "It could use a

little tidying up. Do you have a strong opposition to neatness?"

"On board the *Paradise*, yes," he said easily, hoping he could dislodge her quickly. "I sail to relax and enjoy life—something you might slow down and try to do."

"I enjoy life!" she snapped, and he wondered if she had the foggiest notion of what he meant.

He leaned still closer and took a towel out of her hands. "You've been up here about twenty minutes. Between bites of grilled cheese sandwich, you have stacked up books, and folded a shirt and a towel. Do you know how to relax?"

"Of course I do," Jasmine said, leaning back a fraction. His eyes were a clear sky blue, wide, thickly fringed with lashes, and able to confuse her thought processes with only a glance.

"This is a garbage scow, and I'm just trying to . . ."

"Trying to what?" he asked softly, placing his hands on both sides of her seat, his wrists inches from her thighs.

"How long since you last saw a woman?"

A corner of his mouth lifted in a smile. Matt was amused, intrigued, and pulled by an invisible tension that tightened as he stared into her eyes. Her lips parted slightly, her eyes darkened a fraction, and he felt his temperature climb. Her lips looked soft and inviting, and he wanted to taste them and find out.

"Way too long," he said softly, leaning closer.

"Mr. Rome, I want it clearly understood as of this moment," she paused for a breath, "that you and I are strangers with nothing in common."

Her voice lost its zip. "I have a boyfriend, so please keep your distance."

He thought it over, and then he said, "Okay. And you keep your cleaning instincts to a minimum. Deal?"

"I'll try."

"I'll try too."

To his amusement she scooted away from him, finished her lunch without picking up so much as a slip of paper, and finally carried their dishes back to the galley. He watched her go. He hated to see anything go to waste, and Jasmine Kirby, he decided, was wasting her life. She was young, single, beautiful, and intelligent. She should be enjoying life, not worrying about socks on the deck and papers stowed in a dinghy. If he had been on the *Pelican*, she wouldn't have been set adrift alone.

He glanced in the direction of the small boat, which was secured behind the *Paradise*. With a sigh he stood up and sauntered to the stern. He climbed over the side and into the bobbing dinghy. In twenty minutes he was back at the wheel. His gaze fell on a pile of shells. He got a bucket of water, sat down on a cushion, and began to dip shells into the bucket.

And that was where Jasmine found him when she came above. She paused a moment to look at his bare back. He had a fantastic body, there was no denying it. Maybe it compensated for his lack of ambition. She squared her shoulders and crossed to stand beside him. But not too close beside him. Something happened to her resolve when she got too close.

"I think it's time we unload the dinghy, because

you never know when the weather will change."
She spoke briskly, but all the time she was really
wondering where in Texas he lived.

"I did unload it. Your papers are safe in my
cabin."

He continued what he was working on while
she stared in surprise. She went to the back of
the boat and looked down at the dinghy. It was
empty. He really had unloaded it. Her brows arched,
and she walked over to him, watching him rub
water on a shell.

"What are you doing?"

He tilted his head to look up at her. The cap
was squashed on the back of his head, the frayed,
gray string tangled in his hair. "You inspired me.
I'm cleaning."

"What are you cleaning?" she asked, dismayed
that he would let the whole ship go to pieces while
he scrubbed sand and mud off old seashells.

"This is a shell. Sit down and I'll show it to
you."

"I know it's a shell. If you're going to clean,
shouldn't you start on the ship?"

"Sit down. Let me show you something."

She sat down a foot away from him and folded
her legs under her. He stared at her as she mopped
her brow.

"You're hot."

"It's hot below."

"There's a fan down there. And why don't you
cut the legs off your jeans and get out of that
sweater? I have some T-shirts you can wear."

"Thank you."

"Here." He put down the shell and reached into
the pocket of his cutoffs, leaning back so he could

straighten out enough to dig something out. She wondered how he could carry anything in the pockets of jeans that fit so tightly it seemed a piece of paper couldn't go between them and his body. She looked away, but the image of his narrow hips and the tight denim seemed indelibly stamped on her mind. He produced a knife, flipped it open, and handed it to her. She stared at her jeans, decided he was right, and reached down to cut.

"Hey, that's not the way to do it." He took the knife, moved it inches higher, pinched a bit of material and sliced it neatly. "Stand up. I can do a better job."

"I can—"

"Stand up."

For such a lazy, laid-back man, she thought as she stood up, sometimes he could be quietly in command. He knelt beside her, cutting away. She was acutely aware of his nearness, of his hands brushing lightly against her legs as they moved around to the inside of her thighs. She took a deep breath and wiped her forehead. She felt as if she were on fire, and this time she knew it wasn't because of the sunshine.

"There! Now that should be better." He slit the material he had cut loose and tossed it aside. Then he put away his knife, and motioned to her to sit back down.

He held out a shell to show her. "I got these a long time ago on a beach and I just haven't had time to clean them."

"Time?" She looked at him sharply. "You have all the time in the world! We could be cleaning this deck right now instead—"

It'll keep." He turned the shell. "It's a beauty, isn't it? I always wonder how far the ocean carried it. And what happened to the creature that lived in this shell."

She looked at him as he turned the pink-and-white shell in his big hand, intrigued by his speculations.

"It's lovely and hard and enduring. Yet the animal that lived inside was entirely different from its shell. Soft, often short-lived, slimy—to some repulsive, to some tasty—a creature so different from the shell."

"I hadn't thought about it," she said, curbing the impulse to coil the line that had been tossed down in a heap beside her.

"Look." He rummaged in the pile and pulled out a white sand dollar. "One time I saw two sea urchins eat one of these like a cookie. They had the sand dollar between them and they were slowly devouring it. Look at the center. There's a perfect star."

"I've never looked at one closely," she said, leaning toward him as she peered at the star and the surrounding markings which depicted five petals of a flower.

"Shells are nice," he said in husky tones. She stared into his eyes and forgot about the shell, as tension sparked between them; it was a magic tug that sent a tingle from her head to her toes. She couldn't get her breath and she felt as if she were drowning in a sea of blue. She stood up swiftly. "I think I'll go find one of your T-shirts. I'm on fire."

He smiled slowly, and she blushed, wishing she had worded her remark differently. At that moment a sudden strong gust of wind caught the sails, causing the boat to list. Clothing and towels were swept into the sea.

Jasmine yelped and tried to grab what she could as Matt caught her around the waist to prevent her from falling overboard.

"Hey!"

"Your things went over the side."

"They're replaceable." He moved to change the sails as the cutter heeled sharply again. She stepped back, then scurried into the cockpit. She talked to him as he worked.

"Aren't you going back to pick up your clothes?"

"Nope. There's nothing there of any great value."

"You're littering," she said with annoyance.

He turned around to grin. "I'm *littering* the Atlantic Ocean?"

"Yes, you are! Look at that junk floating around."

"Some fish will eat it by midnight, or some sea creature will make a home in it, and eventually it'll rot. Cities dump garbage in oceans you know."

"Well, it doesn't seem right. And it seems like a silly waste of clothing. I'd think you'd be more careful."

He dropped down into the cockpit where she was, placing his hand on a beam overhead, standing close to her. "But I'm not careful at all when I'm out here. I'm relaxed," he said, and his voice developed that furry rasp that warmed her inside. "I'm content, but I'm not careful."

"No, you're coming on strong. Will you stop?" The next time the wind rose, if everything blew overboard, she would let it go without a remark, she decided.

"Why should I stop?" he asked, arching his

brows. There was a note in his voice that was almost a caress. "You're a beautiful woman, I'm a healthy man."

She dipped to walk under his arm. "I'm hot. I'm getting out of this sweater."

"Need any help?"

"No!"

Ignoring a chuckle, she left and went below, working swiftly to pick up and fold any clothing that looked clean. She selected a white cotton shirt that had a smudge of green paint on the sleeve. With a knife she cut the tail shorter, cut off the collar, and tied the ends high around her waist, sure that Matt Rome wouldn't care what she did to his shirt. She rolled the sleeves high.

Feeling cooler now, she began to clean the stateroom. When she finished, she searched the galley for something to cook for dinner. Her appetite was returning in full force. To her amazement, an ice compartment in the refrigerator held sealed packages of frozen casseroles. She selected a package of chili, while it heated, she got a cold beer for Matt and fixed chocolate milk for herself.

"I thought I heard you in here," Matt said, coming down the companionway. "I'll cook something—" He stopped and looked at her, his eyes drifting slowly over the shirt that was damp now from perspiration and clinging to her full curves. Her nerves quivered in the wake of his glance.

"My shirt never looked better."

"Thanks," she said and laughed.

He smiled. "What's so funny?"

"You. You flirt. Constantly."

"You bring it out in me. I've never done it before." She laughed at that one. Placing her hand on her hip, she studied him. "You're an enigma, Matthew Rome."

"Why?"

"You're lazy, you're sloppy, you're a drifter," she said mildly, "yet sometimes you're neat," she waved at the refrigerator, "and sometimes you're energetic . . ."

"Maybe you're looking more at the shell and not the animal inside," he said, while his gaze went around the galley. He shook his head. "You're trying to straighten me out."

With mock solemnity she shook a spatula at him. "You need to be straightened out and assume a few responsibilities! Don't you ever work?"

His blue eyes twinkled. "Sure, I do. This boat is proof."

"Some proof! Someone probably paid you to haul it away," she said, but there was no anger in her tone. She felt a challenge sparking between them.

"Actually, I won it on a bet."

"That figures. Well, for the few hours that I'm on board, there will be some order to this ship."

"Why?"

"Why?" She laughed at the ridiculous question. "Because it's impossible to live in confusion. It's been human nature since the beginning of the time to create order out of chaos."

"It's also human nature to try to rise above the mundane. And keeping my socks picked up is mundane. There's enough order here. Food is where it should be. The engine works, the sails are in good shape, the hull is watertight—what more could you want?"

"This is a ridiculous way to live! You're walking around on your clean shirts!"

"Jasmine Kirby, you really don't know how to enjoy life," he said softly.

"Let's not argue. I'm heating chili and I have drinks ready."

"Chocolate milk with chili? What's the boyfriend like?" he asked, abruptly changing the subject.

"Boyfriend? Oh, Gary? Gary Hobart. He's head of the team of scientists I work for. He's very efficient, he's intellectual, he's—"

"When was the last time he kissed you?"

She stared at Matt while her merriment changed to irritation, because she couldn't remember. Matt's brows arched and his expression had an "I told you so" smugness to it. "I don't remember, but that isn't important!" she snapped.

"At your age, it should be important," he said, coming toward her.

"You leave—"

His mouth stopped her words. Jasmine's hands flew up to push him away, but her palms landed on a warm, furred chest. His lips parted hers, and she slipped over the edge of protest into a sea of consent.

His tongue was insistent, demanding, probing the recesses of her mouth, the warm moistness of it teasing and inflaming her. Her pulse pounded in her ears as he forced her head to tip back and kissed her deeply one last time.

It was an effort for her to open her eyes. She felt dazed, and excitement raced like summer lightning through her veins.

He stared at her, and she stared back, feeling caught in a whirling current. His expression was solemn. A slight, questioning frown creased his brow. She was breathless, stunned at the reaction he had stirred within her.

"Want to go above and watch the sunset?" he asked quietly. "The wind has died and it's beautiful outside."

She nodded, and he reached over to turn the heat off beneath the chili and quickly set the drinks in the refrigerator. Then he followed her onto the deck. The air was cooler now. A faint teasing breeze came off the water, rippling its surface and tugging at tendrils of Jasmine's hair. They sat on cushions in the cockpit, Matt close beside her, his hip touching hers, as she looked at pink and golden streamers of sunlight dancing across the ocean's surface. She felt dazed, because his kiss had been spectacular. And she was disturbed, because she didn't want an aimless boat bum to be the most spectacular kisser she had ever encountered.

"Whereabouts in Texas do you live?" he asked quietly. She thought he sounded subdued, and she wondered if he had been a little shaken by their kiss too.

"In Houston," she answered. "Where do you live?"

"A little suburban area. When you get back with your group, how long will you stay in Patagonia?" Matt asked, studying her.

"The project is finished, and they had already started home."

"So what will you do?" Matt asked, but his thoughts were only half on his question. He was mulling over the events of the past few minutes. He had been jolted by her kiss. Was it because he had been alone too long? he wondered. Or was there a special chemistry between them? He slanted a look at her. She was staring ahead, looking at the sunset. Her eyelashes were long, thick, and slightly curled. Her skin was flawless and deeply tanned, and he thought he could go on looking at her for a long time. She was a beautiful woman, and his pulse began to accelerate just from watching her.

She ran her hand across her cheek, pushing wayward strands of hair behind her ear. "I'll get an office job. I'm taking correspondence courses in finance now, and I'll probably enroll in night classes."

"You have relatives in Houston?"

She turned to smile briefly at him, then stared out to sea again.

"Yes, my parents. I'm an only child. My father is a pharmacist and my mother is a teacher."

He was surprised at her answer because he had pictured her as part of a big family of busy people. "Did your mother teach you to be so neat?"

Again, she smiled briefly. "Yes, I suppose. Mom and Dad are both neat, and as the only child, I guess it was natural for me to be orderly. What about your family?"

"I have three sisters who live in the States," he said. Shifting the conversation back to Jasmine, he asked, "When did you get the divorce?"

"Eight years ago when I was twenty. I married at nineteen."

"That's young."

"For me, it was too young. What was infatuation and sexual attraction, I thought was love. I was looking for the kind of love and marriage my parents have. I think Chet was looking for a second mother."

"Chet Kirby?"

"No, Kirby is my maiden name. I went back to it."

They were silent for a while, but he leaned back and continued to look at her. In twenty-four hours he would put her ashore and never see her again. And he didn't want to let her go. He thought she needed something more out of life than she was getting. An inner voice laughed at the thought. Matthew Forsythe Rome, knight for distressed damsels. He studied her slender neck, the plait of long dark hair hanging down her back, and for one brief moment he envisioned what she would look like with her hair unbraided, falling free over her bare shoulders. It made his heart thump, and he pursed his lips. Her boyfriend couldn't be all that important to her or their kiss would never have gone on as long as it had. So Matt dismissed the problem of Gary Hobart without a qualm.

"When will you be back in the States?"

"As long as it takes to get to Buenos Aires and then fly home."

"I'm going back to Texas someday. How about a date?"

She turned around to stare at him with wide eyes. She blinked, and the astonishment she felt was so obvious that he almost laughed. He was not accustomed to having a woman react as she did to his request for a date.

Then she smiled, laughed softly, and winked at him. "Sure, Matt, you give me a call."

The wink had done something to his respiratory system. *Give me a call.* He knew she didn't expect ever to hear from him. And he was sure she didn't really think he had meant it. The lady was beautiful and poised and had a busy life. Why did he think she was missing something? And where did he come off thinking he could fill the void? He shook his head while he came to the conclusion that he needed to go ashore and spend an evening in the company of a lovely señorita who was cooperative and exciting. He should tell Jasmine Kirby farewell and let her get on with her life.

And he might have been able to do so, if she had just sat there and looked at the sunset. Instead, at that moment, she sighed, stood up, and said, "It's pretty out here, but I have some laundry soaking. Besides the chili will get cold, and as soon as we eat, I want to tie the records together so we can move them easily tomorrow."

That did it. He stood up swiftly. "Forget about the damned cleaning! The sea is calm and blue, there's a gorgeous sunset here—one the likes of which you seldom get to see—and you're talking about dirty laundry. Don't tell me you know how to enjoy life!"

"I most certainly do! For all you know, laundry is fun!"

"You know what you need? You need to be kissed often and soundly, because it relaxes you. And then you can sit back and enjoy something like a sunset."

"Oh, come on!" she said, laughing. "I've heard lines . . ."

She had laughed at him. He didn't know whether to laugh at himself or kiss her and end the conversation. He opted for the latter. He slipped his arm around her waist, ignoring her protest, which was even briefer than the last time, and placed his mouth on hers. He was lost in a wild eddy of sensation, and she must have been too, because her protests vanished and her arms held him tightly.

When he released her, Jasmine stared at him in shock. His kisses were growing longer, more important, more sensual. She was on fire, and she wanted to close her eyes and pull his head down to kiss him some more, but it was so . . . illogical!

"Come sit down," he said quietly. "I'll get the chili and the drinks."

She did as he asked, watching the sunset. The sky was an explosion of golden rays that sent reflections stretching across the deep blue water. Endless sky and sea spread all around her. The air was clear and pure, and reminded her of days right after heavy rainstorms at home. They could be alone in the whole world, it was so peaceful, she realized. It was quiet, serene . . . except for her pulse. Matt was causing flurries in her heartbeat that she wasn't accustomed to feeling.

While they ate, she sat on the edge of the hammock with her bowl of chili balanced on her lap. He asked again, "How can you drink chocolate milk with chili?"

"I have a weakness for chocolate."

"What else do you have a weakness for?"

"I think that's a loaded question," she said lightly, avoiding giving a direct answer.

"Will you give me your phone number?"

"I'm in the Houston phone directory. Five five five, six seven two one. By the way, if you don't work, how do you buy groceries?"

While he memorized her phone number and tried to keep from staring at her legs, he shrugged, reluctant to tell her all about himself yet. He decided to stick as close to the truth as he could. "If I need something, I can stop in a port and work a little to buy it. Or I can swap something. Sometimes when I find a village and natives that want something I have on board ship, I trade with them."

"You don't get tired of drifting?" she asked, noticing that his fingers were long like an artist's.

"When I get tired of it, I'll quit and go back to Texas."

"And what do you do in Texas?"

"A little of this and a little of that."

Jasmine decided to stop asking him questions about his life. He obviously was a drifter and didn't want to discuss himself. "This is marvelous chili."

"Thank you."

"You made it?"

"Yep. Any Texan worth his salt can cook chili. What's your recipe?"

They compared recipes and decided to have a chili contest someday, and Jasmine began to feel as if she had something warm inside her besides the chili. Matt was fun and exciting and appealing in spite of his goofy hat, fuzzy hair, and scruffy beard. She stopped eating as she remembered his kisses, the most wonderful kisses in her life. The very best. He was gazing at the ocean and holding the beer in his hand, and she studied his profile. His chiseled lips were like velvet. He had strong features and eyes that could send heat through an ice floe. Her gaze returned to his mouth and she touched her tongue to her lips.

He turned and caught her watching him. "What are you thinking about?" he asked softly.

"Nothing," she said, shaking her head and looking down, suddenly embarrassed that he knew what she had been thinking.

"Nothing?"

She raised her head to look him directly in the eye. "Since you have a beer in your hand and chili on your lap, I can safely tell you that I was thinking about your kisses."

"I'll bring the subject up again when we don't have beer and chili between us," he said with a smile, but his voice had lowered a notch, and she realized he responded to her slightest gesture or word. "And you go ahead with the same train of thought."

She shook her head, laughing softly at him. "Not if I can help it."

"My kisses are that disturbing?" he asked, moving aside the almost-empty bowl of chili.

"Matt, finish your chili."

He studied her a moment, then he picked up the bowl and resumed eating. "How did you like Patagonia?"

She sighed, thinking back while she looked at the hypnotic motion of the waves. "It was rugged and barren. I really didn't get to see much because I was in camp transcribing records and cataloging data." She turned and found he was frowning at her.

"Didn't you take time off?" he asked.

"Well, yes. We went into town to eat, and we met some of the local people. That was nice."

"I think you missed something while you were cataloging records," he said softly, almost to himself.

"I'm doing fine. I'm employed, I travel, I'm getting an education for my future career, I date, I have a nice, neat apartment . . . versus . . ." She looked around. "You think studying a pile of seashells is getting a lot out of life?"

He pursed his lips as if he were deep in thought. "Yes, I do. And the location of my socks and shirts doesn't change the quality of my life." He shook his finger at her. "You're looking at the shell again, and not the animal inside."

"Now what do you mean by that? That deep down inside, you're neat and hardworking?"

He grinned. "That might be exactly what I mean."

She shook her head. "There's very little evidence of it! A little, but not enough."

She stood up, picking up both empty bowls. "You live life your way, and I'll"—she paused and winked—"think about what you've said."

His deep chuckle followed her as she carried the dishes below to the galley. He came down to help, and she wished he hadn't. She would have done better alone. In the cramped quarters they continually bumped against each other, and she was growing more disturbed by each contact.

"The galley's clean," he said, taking her hand, as they went to sit in the cockpit. She slipped on her sweater and he pulled on a tattered gray sweatshirt. Then he leaned back beside her.

"Did you ever see such stars?" he asked, slipping his arm around her shoulders. For a moment Jasmine was more aware of his presence than the myriad sparkling dots in the inky sky. She tilted her head back, pressing on his arm, as she gazed above. "It looks as if there are millions more stars than I see at home."

"The air is so clear down here. No pollution—no civilization with lights."

"Look!" There was a flash of brilliant green cutting a swath across the heavens.

"A falling star," he said softly. "We used to wish on them when we were kids."

"Did you wish just then?"

"Yes." His voice was a deep rumble.

"What did you wish?" she asked, curious.

"I wished," he said softly, "that you'd turn around and want me to kiss you."

"I'd never want anyone to fail to get a wish because of me," she whispered, her pulse skipping.

He lifted her chin up, and tightened his arm around her shoulders.

It was a long time before she pushed away, and her voice was breathless as she said, "I think we'd better go back to stargazing."

"Sure," he agreed quietly. "And maybe I'll be in luck and we'll see a meteor shower."

She laughed and moved away a fraction. He kept his arm around her while he pointed out constellations and the bright stars of the Southern Cross.

"Did you go to college?" she asked, still curious about him.

"Yep, a long time ago."

She laughed. "You sound so old!"

"I'm thirty-two. My birthday was yesterday."

"You were out here all alone on your birthday?" she asked, wondering how many birthdays he had spent alone.

"Don't worry. It was a beautiful day and the only way it could have been improved was to have you arrive a day sooner."

"Thank you. Happy birthday, Matthew Rome," she said, still worrying about his solitary life.

"Thanks. You haven't changed your mind about letting me take you home to Texas, have you?"

She shook her head. "No, but thank you. Anyway, I have to get back home to work."

"Anyway—you wouldn't do it no matter what the reason. Okay, I'll take you ashore tomorrow." They sat in silence. She felt as if she were staring into infinity, at endless sky and stars. Waves lapped steadily against the side, creating a gentle rocking motion that was very different from her stormy ride in the dinghy. The white sail was stark against the dark background, and she realized the ship was graceful in spite of the disarray below.

Matt got up to take the wheel and then he worked, adjusting the sail. She relaxed, closing her eyes.

"Where are you going when we part?" she asked.

"Probably head north." He sat down beside her and draped his arm across her shoulders. His voice was a deep rumble in the silence of the night, a pleasant masculine sound that she wanted to go on listening to forever. "You said you'll be looking for another job. I know of a temporary one. A friend of mine in Texas has some old family diaries and letters of historical importance. He hasn't had time to sort them out and he wants to get them organized. He needs a good efficient secretary. Think you might be interested?"

She smiled. "Thanks, Matt, but I doubt if that would pay as well as an office job. It sounds like something he can get someone to do as part-time work."

"If I see him, do you care if I give him your phone number? He might pay more than you think."

"Sure. I'd better go below. I'm exhausted."

"You can't go down and sleep in the cabin. It's like climbing down into a cave. You can have the hammock and I'll sleep on the cushions. I promise to keep my distance."

"We'd be all of two feet apart, and I've never slept in a hammock. The cabin is fine. I cleaned it today."

"Get ready to turn in and come back up here. I'll have a sleeping bag for you in the hammock, and I swear I'll be on my best behavior. Look at the sky and the moon. It's a perfect night."

She glanced at the panorama overhead. Matt's fingers drifted across the nape of her neck at that moment, and common sense evaporated. "Okay, you win!"

She went below and returned a few minutes later still wearing the cutoffs and sweater. Her hair was unbraided, falling loosely over her shoulders.

Three

"I've got the sails set for the night," Matt said. "There's a self-steering device on the wheel to keep us on course. Here's—you unbraided your hair," he said in a voice that was as soft and warm as fur. He held her away to look at her, then pulled her close as he slipped his arms around her waist. "It's been a fun evening. I'm sorry the *Pelican* sank, but I'm glad you're here."

"Thank you. You'll never know how glad I was to find you!"

"Even if I'm Charlie Allnutt?"

"You're a great Charlie Allnutt. Helpful, resourceful, unforgettable."

"Ah, I hope so. You're a little unforgettable yourself, Jasmine Kirby." He leaned closer as he talked and ran one hand through the black cascade of her hair. "You're beautiful."

She didn't hear the last of his words. What she felt when she was around him was magic, more mystifying and sparkling than the stars above.

His lips touched hers lightly, making hers tingle and want more. He kissed the corner of her mouth and, as her lips parted, she turned her head a fraction and their lips met. His arms tightened around her, and he bent over her, molding her against him while his tongue thrust deeply into her mouth.

Jasmine trembled with desire. Flames curled along her veins and she clung to him, returning his kisses with abandon. She felt his body's response, his hard maleness pressing against her. He stroked the nape of her neck, his hand drifting around to the side of her neck. With effort, she moved away.

"Matt, we should stop now," she said shakily. "Are you all right?"

"Yeah," he said in a strained voice.

She climbed into the sleeping bag on the hammock. Lying back, she stared overhead at a breathtaking view of the night sky, while her thoughts remained on Matt Rome, his spectacular body, and his fiery kisses. She had to admit he was fun and intriguing. She turned to find him stretched out only a short distance away from her on the cushions. He'd pulled a light blanket over himself.

" 'Night," he said in a tone that was as disturbing as the touch of his hand.

" 'Night, Matt. Thanks for rescuing me."

"I'm still trying to rescue you, Jasmine," he said huskily. She stared at him, her eyes narrowing. She decided she hadn't heard him correctly and went back to looking at the stars.

"Isn't this beautiful?" he asked.

"Yes," she said, becoming more and more aware

of his long, powerful body so close to hers. "I have to sleep. I'm exhausted."

" 'Night," he whispered again.

The next morning Jasmine awoke when the sun was already angled above the horizon. The wind was brisk, giving the ship more motion than it had the day before, but the sun was bright and the sky was dotted with white clouds like snow-balls thrown against a blue coat. When she stood up, the cutter listed, a wave hit, and cold, white spray fell like mist on her face. She rubbed her cheeks and went below to wash, learning to walk with the movement of the ship. When she returned she found Matt in the cockpit.

"Good morning."

The cap was pushed down on his forehead. He wore his cutoffs and a sweatshirt with the sleeves pushed high. He stood up, his strong legs spread slightly apart to steady himself against the rocking of the boat. His gaze drifted down like fingers touching her in a lingering caress.

Trying to ignore the swift reaction she had to his look, she held out her hand. She shook her long braid behind her head as she said, "Happy birthday!"

He gave her a startled glance, and took from her hand the tiny package wrapped in newspaper and bound with a rubber band.

"I found the newspaper in the cabin," she said, bracing her hip against the bulkhead. "It was under a pair of dusty boots and it's three months old, so I didn't think you were saving it."

"I wasn't." He opened the paper and looked down at the plastic black-and-white penguin pin she had been wearing on her sweater when she came aboard. "It's for your hat." She took his cap and pinned the penguin on the side.

He accepted the hat and admired the pin. "That's great! That's really great!" he exclaimed with unnecessary enthusiasm. "What a nice surprise." He placed it on his head and turned for her approval. "How's it look?"

"Perfect," she said, looking at his blond hair, which was sticking out in tangles from beneath the wrinkled old cap. The silly frayed string now hung behind his head.

He grinned. "How very nice and thoughtful. I have to thank you properly." He wrapped his arms around her and kissed her long and hard, until her thoughts were jumbled. Suddenly, the *Paradise* tilted and they both almost fell.

"Matt!" She scooted out of his grasp. "What would you do if I gave you something valuable?" she asked with a laugh.

"You did give me something valuable. The pin is super." His smile made her glow.

"Have you had breakfast?"

"Yep. Hours ago while you lolled in the sun, yet I'm the one called lazy."

She blushed. "Sor—"

"Ah, regrets!"

They laughed together, and then she went below to get her breakfast.

At midday gulls appeared, circling high, then swooping to the water, their wings spread gracefully. When Matt told her their appearance meant land was near, she felt a growing twinge of disappointment. She sat in the cockpit washing shells while he adjusted the sails. The weather had warmed. She wore his shirt, and he was barechested again, his back muscles rippling as he worked.

She was tempted to tell him she would sail north with him and let him take her back to Texas. The thought made her heart jump, but as quickly as the notion came, she squelched it. She had to get back to Texas as soon as possible and find a job and get enrolled in night classes. And if she sailed north with Matt, she might be madly in love with him by the time they reached Texas. As appealing and exciting as Matt was, he didn't look the type to settle down or take on a shred of responsibility, and she didn't want to lose her heart to a drifter today any more than she had wanted to yesterday.

She had to admit that he had one of the most spectacular bodies she had ever seen, and she found it fascinating to watch him move around. He was bent over, securing a line to a cleat, his body, arms and legs making an arc. Suddenly he turned his head and looked into her eyes. He smiled, and she winked. Then she went back to washing a shell, wondering why she was cleaning shells instead of the galley or the deck.

Gradually the speck in the distance took shape. Solid land spread across the horizon. She could make out the dark sand, a small dock, and a tiny town. Civilization—and farewell to Matthew Rome.

She didn't want to part from him, but the time had come. He had radioed ahead and received a reply that the others from the *Pelican* had gone ashore at Río Gallegos. They would come by bus to Bahía Grande to meet her, and mail the records back to Texas. Then they would all take the bus to Buenos Aires and fly home. They didn't expect to get to Bahía Grande until midafternoon, so she knew she might have several hours to wait.

Matt went ashore with her and took her to lunch at a small restaurant on a dusty backstreet. The walls were stucco, and there were pots of flowers everywhere. They sat in a cool room that had rough beams across the low ceiling. She let Matt order for her in Spanish while she watched him with amusement. He had placed his hat on another chair and he wore a T-shirt and his cutoffs. Combing his hair with his fingers had been his concession to grooming, but she noticed that his long fingers were spotlessly clean, the nails blunt and trimmed.

He ordered *pollo borracho* for both of them, and as soon as they were alone, she asked him what it was.

" 'Drunken chicken.' It's a typical dish, made of chicken and ham in a casserole with white wine. And we'll have rice with it. Okay?"

"Sounds great." They smiled at each other for a long moment. His eyes were deep, clear blue fringed with thick golden lashes, sexy eyes.

"I hope we cross paths again," he said, taking her hand and smoothing her slender fingers in his palm.

"That would be nice. It'll have to be in Texas, because I won't be back here."

"Now how do you know what tomorrow will bring?"

"Until this trip I'd never been out of the Southwest," she said, looking at her hand dwarfed by his. With his forefinger he traced an invisible line over her knuckles. His hand was tanned, freckled, and covered with golden hair, and she found it more attention-consuming than their conversation. "This job was unusual," she said. "And my life normally follows the usual."

"I don't know about that. You were shipwrecked and rescued, and here you are in Patagonia eating drunken chicken. That's usual?"

She laughed, feeling an abiding happiness with him, a feeling she didn't want to look at too closely or think about because soon they would part forever.

"I'll always wonder whether you would have sailed with me back to Texas if I'd had a yacht and it had been neat and clean and tidy."

She shook her head. "No. I have to find a job. Where was the last place you worked?"

He shrugged his broad shoulders. "I did a little flying for some people."

Before she could comment, their waiter returned with steaming dishes of food. Jasmine thought the chicken was delicious; it tasted doubly marvelous after the sparse meals she'd had on board the *Paradise*.

"This is wonderful!"

"I wish you had worked up that much enthusiasm for the *Paradise*!"

"Drunken chicken is special," she said, finishing the last bite.

He smiled and asked, "Ready to go?"

She nodded and stood up. Walking ahead of him, she realized she wanted to prolong their last moments together. On the dock a dark-skinned boy approached, Polaroid camera in hand, and talk to Matt in rapid Spanish. Matt answered, bargained briefly, then stepped beside her and slipped his arm around her waist.

"He wants to take our picture. Smile."

"Won't it cost money?" she asked, worried about his finances.

"Not much." As soon as the first picture was snapped, Matt's arm tightened around her waist. "Stand still. We need two. One for you and one for me. I want you to remember the *Paradise*."

She laughed, and waited for the second snapshot. As soon as Matt paid him, the boy handed over the pictures. She stood close to Matt, and she caught the scent of his woodsy aftershave while she looked at the pictures. "Here's yours."

"Thanks," she said, knowing she wouldn't forget him whether she had his picture or not.

When she climbed on board, he pulled her around to face him. "I have a present for you. I might not get to give it to you later when your friends arrive." He went inside, then came right back. "Here—my favorite shell." He held out the pink-and-white shell and she accepted it, turning it in her palm.

"I love it!" she exclaimed. "When I look at it I'll think of you," she said, looking into his eyes. She was ensnared by invisible chains that bound some part of her to him. For a moment her feeling of regret over their parting was intense, then it was replaced by desire, which she saw mirrored in his expression.

He took the shell from her and placed it carefully on the deck. Then he enfolded her in his arms as he leaned back against the bulkhead, spreading his legs apart and pulling her tightly to his broad chest. While he kissed her passionately, his hands drifted down her back, over the sloping curve of her buttocks. He pulled her closer, fitting her to him. She felt his hard arousal and it caused an instant response within her. Her hips moved and she burned with passion.

She twisted free and moved away, her breathing as labored as if she had just run a race. "We should stop or you'll get hurt."

"I'm all right," he said solemnly, his breathing as ragged as hers.

Before she could reply, she heard the rumble of an automobile.

A flatbed truck approached, the gray body spotted with rust, an occasional patch of the original white paint still clinging to the metal. Dust blew off the back of the bed as the truck bumped along. When Gary Hobart leaned out the passenger window, she waved to him.

"There's Gary!" she cried, hurrying to meet him. The truck stopped, and a man stepped down.

Matt followed slowly, pausing at the edge of the deck. He squinted, looking at a man who resembled a dark-eyed Tom Selleck. Momentarily, Matt wondered if he should have told Jasmine more about himself. As he looked at the handsome man, who was dressed in neat khakis and boots, Matt regretted he hadn't worn something different, but as swiftly as the notion came, he rejected it. If he had to live the past two days over again, he would do everything the same.

Jasmine walked into Gary's waiting arms, and he hugged her. To Matt's enormous relief, she turned her cheek and they didn't kiss. It was amazingly painful for him just to see her hug another man. She turned and the driver came around the front of the truck to give her a brief, quick squeeze. She said something to them, and all three looked at Matt. He forced a polite smile and walked to meet them.

"Matt, this is Gary Hobart and Tim O'Rourke. Guys, this is Matt Rome who rescued me."

"That's great. We had bad luck with the old *Pelican*," Gary said, as he gave Matt a smile and a firm handshake.

"We were worried sick about Jasmine. She's been the glue that's held everything together on this expedition," Tim said.

"So I'm glue?" she asked teasingly.

"Glue and pure gold. I hear you saved the records."

"That we did," she answered, glancing at Matt.

"We've latched onto a truck," Gary said. "Rented it for the afternoon, so we'll load up our records and be on our way."

Jasmine helped the men carry the papers and ledgers to the truck, then retrieved the shell Matt had given her. Matt shook hands with them and they all said good-bye, while Gary waited with his hand on Jasmine's arm.

She offered her hand. "Bye, Matt."

"Good-bye, Jasmine."

She walked away from him, and he felt as if he were losing something valuable. He had been telling women good-bye off and on all his adult life. He couldn't recall a time when it had hurt as it did now, and it seemed ridiculous because he had only known Jasmine two days. Ridiculous or not, each step she took away from him increased a panicky feeling inside him that he wouldn't see her again. As they reached the truck, he called to her.

"Jasmine!"

She turned around, said something to Gary, and came back to meet him halfway as he crossed the pier. "Five five five, six seven two one?" he asked so softly no one else could possibly hear.

"Good memory!" she said with a wink.

She hurried back to the truck, waved, and then they were gone.

Matt stared after them until the truck was out of sight, wondering how someone he had known so briefly could cause such a disturbance in his life. Returning to the *Paradise*, he studied his charts, checked on the weather conditions to the north, and got ready to go by motor instead of sail. He wanted to get the *Paradise* as far north as Comodoro Rivadavia. He could dock there, and get Leo to fly down in a company plane and take the *Paradise* back to Texas. Matt tried to avoid thinking about Jasmine traveling with Gary Hobart. There wasn't a strong attraction between the two, Matt already knew that, but the thought didn't reassure him.

He pulled off his cap, looked at the penguin pin, and laughed at himself. When was the last time he had been in a dither over a woman? He remembered Jasmine's sea-green eyes, her kisses, her silky black hair. More important than her looks had been the sudden surfacing at odd moments of her good humor, and the surprising ease he felt being with her. He sailed to relax and to be alone, and he had never brought a woman on board the *Paradise.* He grinned, imagining what Jasmine would say were he to admit *that* to her, but he had not only enjoyed Jasmine's companionship, he missed her now. She had accepted him for himself, and that was something that really mattered, he thought somberly.

While he thought about her and wondered if he would feel the same about her under other circumstances, he worked faster. He wanted to be in Texas as soon as she was, because he intended to get to know Jasmine Kirby very well.

Jasmine bounced on the seat of the truck between Gary and Tim, while they told her what had happened to them. They had been caught in the rain, and when it stopped they had fired a flare, watching for one from her until another cloudburst made them pull the tarp over their heads. At dawn they had rowed west. In a short time had sighted land, and from then on everything had been routine.

She listened to them talk, but her mind and heart were elsewhere. She had only known Matt for two days and one night, but each moment stood out in her memory with the same intense, vivid clarity of the stars in the previous night's sky. She missed him and wished she would see him again someday. She turned the shell in her hand while the men talked, and she thought about Matt. The picture was in the back pocket of her cutoffs, tucked safely away and out of sight. Facing reality, she didn't expect ever to see him again.

All through the journey to Buenos Aires, and

then on to Houston, she still ached from a steady, persistent longing. And her relationship with Gary had undergone a change. She didn't feel the same easygoing friendship with him or the attraction to him she had experienced before, but they were too busy to bring it into the open between them.

During the first hour she was home, she called her parents. The phone rang four times before her mother answered and said a breathless hello.

"Mom, I'm home," she said, looking around at her pink-and-white bedroom with its old-fashioned iron bed she had found in a secondhand store and painted white. The café curtains were frilly and white and allowed sunshine to pour in through the south windows.

"Jasmine! Oh, we're glad you're back."

"You sound out of breath."

"I just came in from school. The phone was ringing when I unlocked the door. How was your trip home?"

"Eventful," Jasmine said, taking Matt's picture out of her pocket and studying it, staring at his bold features, his thick, golden hair and his strong nose. She wondered where he was sailing at the moment and what he was doing.

"Jasmine, are you there?"

"Oh, sure! Mom, the *Pelican* sank."

"I read about it in the newspapers."

"You knew?" Jasmine asked, startled. She looked at her neat room, imagining how Matt would view it and say, "Miss Efficiency." It was neat and tidy, books lined up on her desk and in straight rows on the bookshelves along one wall.

"Yes, Dad and I knew about it, but the account we read in the paper said everyone was safe."

"I didn't call from Argentina because I didn't want to worry you, but I didn't think that the story would make the paper."

"It said there was a fire."

"There was, and we did get off in time. I was in a small boat, and when we were caught in a rainstorm, I got separated from the others."

"You were alone?"

"I was fine, Mom. Really. The next day I crossed paths with a ship and was rescued."

"Oh, Jasmine, thank goodness I didn't know! Were you terrified?"

"It was just one night. Gary had said we'd all be picked up the next morning or get to shore somehow."

"Was it a foreign ship or American?"

"It was owned by a Texan."

"A Texan? One man?"

"Yes. Matthew Rome."

"My word! What was he doing out alone on the Atlantic?"

"He sails."

"All the time?"

"I think so."

"The important thing is he rescued you. Since he's from Texas, I hope I get a chance to thank him some day."

"I hope you do too," Jasmine said sincerely. "But I don't think he comes home much."

"Was it a big, safe boat?"

"It was *Paradise*. That was the name," she added hastily. "The *Paradise*." She put down the picture and picked up the shell Matt had given her. "He was an interesting man."

"I imagine so. Come over for dinner and you can tell us all about it."

"Thanks, Mom. See you soon."

She hung up the phone and flopped back on the bed to stare at Matt's picture again. "Where are you now, Matthew Rome?"

She could imagine him sailing, the wind blowing his laundry overboard, and she smiled, feeling a pang of longing that was ridiculous. She had been with him too short a time for him to make such an impression on her—it was as if he had taken some part of her heart and soul, leaving her not quite whole.

The ringing of the phone interrupted her thoughts and she picked up the receiver to hear Gary's cheerful voice.

"Hi. We can finally be alone. How about dinner tomorrow night?"

"That would be nice," she said cautiously, looking at the smiling blue eyes in the shiny picture.

"I've got to run now. I have another meeting in ten minutes. They're trying to get a campaign started to get donations for another boat. I hope it's better than the *Pelican*."

"It couldn't be much worse!" she said, laughing.

"That's right. How about seven?"

"Fine."

"See you then."

The phone clicked and she sat staring thoughtfully into space. She wasn't as eager to go out with Gary as she had been before she had met Matt. But she had to try to learn exactly what she did feel for Gary—and if she didn't want to continue seeing him, she had to tell him. All the way back on the long trip home, she hadn't felt any more attraction or friendship for him than for the others in the group. And that was a decided change from before. And it was ridiculous! She shouldn't let Matt Rome interfere in her life when she wouldn't see him again. She turned the picture face down on the table and began to unpack furiously, but all the time her thoughts kept straying, remembering him.

She ate dinner with her parents and told them some things about Matt. When she showed them his picture, they thought it was a shame they couldn't meet him and thank him. And Jasmine thought so too. The next night, she dressed in a red sweater and skirt and waited for Gary to pick her up.

She was ready before he came, and she moved restlessly around her small living room. Wood was stacked neatly in the fireplace. Her mother had watered her hanging plants while she had been in South America. She ran her finger along the arm of the beige chintz sofa and looked at the tidy room, which had prints of flowers on the walls. It seemed empty and a little devoid of character. She placed the shell on the center of the mantelpiece, and decided to use a part of her paycheck to buy different prints, pictures of the sea. The doorbell rang and she went to greet Gary.

She had left Argentina the last week of February, the end of the summer in the southern hemisphere, the end of winter in Texas. She stepped outside into a cool, March night. Gary wore a brown sweater and slacks, and excitement shone in his expression as he talked about the enthusiasm the people at the university had for their summer project.

They went to an Italian restaurant. Over candle-light, a red-checked tablecloth, and plates of hot, thick, red meat sauce on buttery white spaghetti, she talked with Gary about their trip. And as she looked into his dark eyes, she knew their relation-ship was over. The spark was gone, extinguished totally by Matt.

Gary talked about the new plans the group was making, and while she listened, she studied him. By ordinary standards, he was far more hand-some than Matt Rome. Gary's features weren't as rugged, he wasn't scarred, he had a straight, thin nose, and his neatly combed brown hair wasn't in a constant tangle. He had muscles and broad shoulders and was just as tall as Matt. He was fun and intelligent, *but not as much fun.* He didn't make her stop and look at the world as if it were a brand-new gift. And his kisses didn't melt every bone in her body. She realized her mind had drifted, and she tried firmly to concentrate on Gary's discussion of how they intended to raise funds for a new boat.

As they ate, they also talked about her future plans, and finally when their empty plates had been removed and they sat with cups of hot coffee in front of them, he folded his arms on the table and leaned closer.

"Something's changed, hasn't it?" he asked quietly.

"Yes." She had to admit the truth.

He tilted his head to one side. "Was it because I let you drift off alone?"

"Heavens, no! Of course not! I told you that when we were in Argentina. You couldn't help what happened. I—"

"I hated it," he said. "I worried about you. We all did, but I felt so damned responsible."

"Oh, Gary, it's not that at all! Don't blame yourself—my word, you fell in the ocean."

"That was the coldest water I've ever been in." He sat in silence for a moment, looking at her. "If you're not angry over being alone—is it the guy who rescued you?"

"That's perceptive of you. Yes. I'm sorry."

"I'm sorry, too, but we'll stay friends, won't we?"

"Of course," she said, smiling at him.

He shrugged. "I'm leaving on a trek to the Himalayas in three weeks. We wouldn't have had much time anyway."

She felt relieved even though she knew Gary wasn't particularly hurt. He was busy, and they hadn't been strongly attracted.

"Are you ready to go?"

"Yes," she answered. When they reached her front door, he kissed her lightly and smiled.

"It's been great. I'm glad you went with us. Oh, we're getting T-shirts that read, 'I survived the *Pelican*.' I'll send you one."

"Thanks."

"I guess yours should read, 'I survived the *Pelican* all by myself.' " He paused. "Bye, Jasmine," he said warmly. "Tell Matthew Rome hello for me when you see him."

" 'Night, Gary. Thanks for the dinner, and good luck on your trip."

"Yeah, thanks." He kissed her again on the

cheek and turned to go. She went inside and closed the door, leaning against it, feeling a forlorn emptiness. *Tell Matthew Rome hello.*

She wouldn't see Matthew Rome. And now she wouldn't see Gary. She looked around the empty apartment. "Good going, Jasmine," she said aloud and walked straight to the bedroom to pick up Matt's picture.

The corner of the photo was bent slightly, but it didn't affect the picture. She held it under the light. "You're causing a lot of trouble in my life, mister!" She plopped down on the pink cotton bedspread to stare at his picture. "Come back to Texas," she whispered, knowing how futile her wish was.

To her amazement, the ache didn't lessen after she had settled into a routine at home in Houston. Matt Rome was like sunshine. She had stepped too close and been changed forever. Some part of her had melted and re-formed into a different shape. She wasn't as efficient as before. Her mind wandered when she filled out job applications. Worse, a couple of times during a job interview her thoughts had drifted. She noticed more of her surroundings, things as simple as pine trees, she now stopped to admire, thinking about their beauty, knowing that it was something Matt would appreciate.

After a long day with two interviews, she came home to her small apartment and heard her phone ringing. Expecting the caller to be her mother or one of her friends, she picked up the receiver.

"Jasmine, this is Matt Rome."

Her heart lurched and she gripped the phone tighter. "Where are you?"

"Here. In Houston." Her heart began to pound with eagerness as she listened to him. "I told you I'd be back in Texas. I asked you for a date, remember."

"Yes, I remember," she said, closing her eyes and smiling. How could she forget? She wanted to jump in the air and kick her heels!

"Want to go to dinner tonight?"

"Tonight?" she repeated in dismay. "I'd love to," she answered quickly. While they talked a few minutes longer and she gave him her address and directions on how to find her apartment, her mind raced over what she would have to do to get ready to go out and what she could wear.

In her mind she pictured Matt in his tattered, faded cutoffs, his battered hat, and sneakers. "You made incredibly fast time sailing back to Texas," she said in awe.

She heard the amusement in his voice when he answered. "I used the motor."

"Motor! You had a motor?"

"I never said I didn't."

"But you knew I wanted to get back to shore as quickly . . ." Her voice faded away because her protest was absurd now. She'd had a grand time with him.

"I'd been alone for weeks, and suddenly a beautiful woman appeared out of nowhere," he said in a voice as soft as velvet. "Now you really can't blame me for not mentioning a motor. I wanted to have dinner with you. I motored to Comodoro Rivadavia and hopped a flight home to Texas. I got you to Ba—"

"Matt, I'm glad you didn't tell me about the motor."

"I wish there wasn't a phone and distance between us now," he said softly, and she tumbled down on the bed and picked up the picture that was on the table. She stared at his image while he asked, "How's the job hunting?"

"Fine, I guess. I don't have a job yet." She didn't tell him she was having difficulty interviewing because of him.

They talked for a while about inconsequential things, her interviews, her trip home, his trip north in the *Paradise*. As soon as she was off the phone, she decided to wear something simple and plain, debating a moment before she selected a dusty pink sweater and fully pleated matching pink wool skirt. She hurriedly straightened the apartment, thankful she had replaced the flower prints in the living room with two of sailing ships at sea. She had bought some colorful throw pillows for the beige sofa, and for a moment she paused to look things over, deciding the small touches were an improvement.

While she bathed, she hummed a tune. Matt was here in Houston!

Could he afford to take her to dinner? She didn't care how simple it was; she wanted to see him. By the time she had looped and pinned her hair on top of her head and pulled on high-heeled white leather boots, her pulse was skipping as merrily as leaves in the wind.

She selected a gold chain to wear around her neck and dangling gold earrings. With a touch of perfume, she was ready. As she went through the living room, she paused to pick up the shell Matt had given her. She ran her finger across its ridges, thinking she had changed since she met him.

Time didn't exist with Matt. She had known him briefly, but he had affected her profoundly. And any minute she would be with him!

The doorbell rang and she put down the shell and eagerly hurried to open the door. Matt stood on the doorstep and her heart stopped as she stared at him in shock.

Four

She felt something like a blow to her midsection when she looked into his blue eyes, but then her gaze flicked over him, and shock reverberated through her in waves. She paused to look at him slowly. Her amazement mounted as she took in short, neatly feathered and combed blond hair, a clean-shaven face, a snowy white shirt, a dark tie, and a charcoal suit cut western style. His clothes fit perfectly, right down to the shiny-toed black western boots he wore. Matt was devastatingly handsome, but the transformation in his apparel might as well have been a flashing neon sign proclaiming that he was a different Matt Rome!

As if he could read her thoughts, he said quietly, "I'm the same guy you met on the *Paradise*."

She was too stunned to answer for a moment. "Why did you let me think . . ." Her words faded.

"That I was a boat bum? Part of me *is* a boat bum. If you didn't like that part—we might as well find out right off. Can I come in?"

"Oh!" Startled, she realized she had been staring, and had left him standing in a chilly wind. She looked into his eyes and felt shy. Yet she knew that had he appeared in jeans and a cotton shirt, she probably would have welcomed him with a hug.

He entered the short hallway, and she closed the door behind him. "This is a very small apartment," she said, still in shock, feeling as if she were with a total stranger. "Here's the living room."

Like a cat in new surroundings, he moved around the room slowly. "It's nice," he said, looking quickly at the bookshelves on both sides of the fireplace, the framed prints of the ships, the shell on the center of the mantel. He moved around the sofa and stopped at the bookcase to pick up a picture of a child. "Who's this?"

Momentarily forgetting her astonishment, she crossed the room to stand beside him. "Those are my children." At his curious glance, she added, "Not really mine, of course. You've seen those magazine ads about adopting a foster child? These are my two. I send a little money each month. The agency sent the pictures. The little one is Maria. The other one is Nagata."

"That's nice, Jasmine," he said, and she turned around to face him. He was only a few feet away, and she was enveloped in a warm look that made her feel as if she were slowly melting. He held out his arms, and she walked into them without hesitation, slipping hers around his neck. Their lips met, touching lightly, sweetly, then he raised his head to look at her. "I missed you," he said, and his head dipped down again, and this time he kissed her passionately. Like a sweeping ocean wave, longing surged up through her body, drowning her in sensation. She kissed him in return. Whatever the changes—he was still Matt.

When he released her, she stared at him. "You have some explaining to do."

"I can do it over dinner." He held her away to look at her, and his voice lowered a notch as he said, "You look beautiful."

"Thank you," she answered, but she was awed by the change in him, and her curiosity was growing.

"I'm still Matt—just dressed differently."

"I'll wait until all the facts are in before I give my opinion."

"Yes, ma'am!" They both laughed, and he helped her on with her coat before taking her hand to go.

The restaurant was located on several sprawling acres of beautiful grounds. There was a pond, and peacocks ambled slowly beneath tall pines. As soon as they were alone, Matt said, "I'm employed and I earn a decent living."

She had a feeling that was the understatement of the year. His suit looked tailor-made.

"I own Rome Aerospace, Incorporated, a plant that does aircraft design, testing, engineering, maintenance, and sales. Small jets are the mainstay of the company."

"How did you get into the airplane business?" she asked, overcome with curiosity about him.

"I loved to fly when I was a kid. My uncle had a little hangar where he rented space to people. He did repairs and gave flying lessons. He taught me how to fly when I was fourteen. I grew up wanting to be in the business. I inherited his hangar and expanded it as the business grew."

She listened to him talk, but she was still overwhelmed that he had kept the truth from her and let her think he was a bum. "Why didn't you tell me?"

He shrugged. "I found it rather novel to have someone like me solely for myself, sort of in spite of what you thought I was."

She understood instantly. He had rugged features, but with his physique and masculine appeal, he was crowd-stoppingly handsome. She knew that the combination of his wealth and his appearance would cause some women to be more than nice to him for reasons that would suit their own purposes.

"Forgive me?" Matt asked, staring at her and holding his breath.

He looked genuinely worried, and she smiled, wanting to push the table aside, to be in his arms. "I forgive you—it isn't important, except that I don't know anything about you."

"Ah, Jasmine," he said softly, sounding so pleased that her heart began to drum in a swifter beat, and it increased another degree as he leaned across the table to kiss her lightly on the mouth.

"Matt!"

He smiled, and sat back as the waiter appeared to take their orders. While he gave both orders, Matt felt enormously relieved because she hadn't been angry; she seemed to understand his feelings and accept his actions. He knew he should have leveled with her on the boat, but there had been too many women he had dated who were more interested in what he owned and what he did than in him personally. It had been refreshing to find someone like Jasmine. And she wasn't on the warpath because he hadn't told her everything at the start! He wanted to pull her into his arms and kiss her until she fainted. A steady, burning warmth inside him made him fight back a grin.

As soon as the waiter left, she said, "Tell me more about yourself."

He began to talk, but his mind was on her instead of on what he was saying. She looked so beautiful, it was all he could do to keep his hands to himself. The dusty pink was a perfect foil for her dark beauty, and when she looked at him, his breathing became irregular. His reactions to her were ridiculous. He couldn't think of a single woman who had stirred him so deeply. The knowledge intrigued him while a little cynical part of him kept waiting for the moment when his interest would wane. His gaze lowered to skim over her full curves. She was scrubbed, combed, flawlessly neat, and tempting. He wanted to take her hair down, remembering how she had looked that night on the *Paradise*. Finally, having tried to exercise patience and wait until the right moment, he brought up the subject he had wanted to talk about earlier.

"I'm the friend who wants some old papers organized and transcribed."

"How many more surprises do you have for me?"

"Well, now—"

"Never mind!" she said, her voice full of laughter.

He sat back and smiled, feeling inordinately pleased with her. She was turning out to be all he had hoped and dreamed about on the trip home. "Actually I want the content of the notes put on a computer and the actual chronicles and papers put together neatly to give to a museum."

Jasmine's heart jumped. She had dismissed his mention of his friend without further thought because she hadn't expected to apply for the job. Now she listened, because it was Matt asking her to become his employee. As badly as she wanted to work for him, she shook her head. "I might do it part-time, but I have to have a job with a certain amount of income."

"What did you get in your last office job?" he asked matter of factly, and when she told him, without hesitation he said, "I'll double that amount."

First, she stared at him; second, she laughed. "That's absurd! I'll go out with you. You don't have to pay a king's ransom for my company!"

"I'm not kidding." He leaned back as the waiter placed crystal dishes of crisp green salad in front of them. As soon as they were alone, Matt continued, "I can afford it. I want someone I can trust, someone who is competent, and since the job entails staying at my ranch—"

"Hey!" Her green eyes flashed with fire. "You should've learned on your boat." She stared down as if she were thinking of the right words, then she raised her head and looked him straight in the eye, lifting her chin defiantly. "I'm not the type for casual affairs. The money isn't any compensation. I'm not the woman you want for the job—or to put it bluntly, I won't go to bed with you unless I feel there is love and a deep, abiding commitment between us. I'm old enough now to know what I want."

"I wasn't asking you to go to bed," he said calmly, trying to keep from smiling.

"There isn't any other reason you would pay me that much!" she snapped.

"Whoa!" he said with a laugh. "You're getting angrier by the second, and all I've done is make you a good business offer. If I were a perfect stranger would you answer the same way?"

"A perfect stranger wouldn't make me an offer like you have! And if he did, I'd probably tell him to get lost!"

He laughed again, getting more amused at the predicament he was getting himself into by merely trying to hire her. "You called me lecherous and lazy before, and I might have been lazy and a little lecherous, but I didn't do anything on the *Paradise* against your wishes—remember?"

Suddenly, she laughed. "You're hopeless!"

"Hell, no. I want to hire you as my secretary." He leaned forward. "Look, my great-great-grandmother was a Comanche. She married a frontiersman."

"You couldn't be part Comanche with your blond hair and blue eyes!"

"Yes, I am, and I can prove it. My ancestors were Comanche and Spanish. There are plenty of blond, blue-eyed Spaniards. Besides, that was generations ago. As I was saying, this is early Texas history and it should go into university archives or a museum, or be compiled into a book for publication by a university press. Here," he said, reaching in his coat pocket, "I had a feeling I might have difficulty convincing you of the honesty and sincerity and goodness of my motives, so I brought you a page from one of my relatives' journals."

She accepted the yellowed, tattered paper from him and while he ate his salad she read: *"Novem-*

*ber, 1846. Some of us decided to have a buffalo
hunt because we had been told that buffalo
were plentiful just south of the Brazos river.
Knowing we would be gone for some time, we
packed provisions, good guns and good horses,
and plenty of water and ammunition. It took
four days to reach the edge of the buffalo range.*

*"We found a large herd grazing near the river.
We had been told it is impossible to get close
enough on foot to shoot them, so we agreed to
hunt on horseback. A charge was ordered and
as we bore down on them, the herd began to
run. They scattered in all directions, and our
guns went off in all directions. I thought my
horse, as well as myself, would get trampled . . ."*

She came to the end of the page and returned it
to him.

"Does that calm some of your fears?"

"It adds to my curiosity," she replied quietly.

"About what?" He folded the page in his long
fingers and slipped it into his pocket.

"About you." She paused while plates of wild
rice and broiled lobster tails with melted butter
were placed in front of them. When the waiter had
left, she said, "This looks delicious."

"And you look like a cat in a new home. What
are you curious about?"

"Your family. You evaded questions on the
Paradise, and I dropped the subject."

He smiled at her, noticing how the reflection of
the flickering candlelight made golden fires in the
green depths of her eyes. He wanted to make her
smile, to hear her laugh. And more than he could
remember wanting anything in a long, long time,

he wanted to talk her into coming to the ranch with him.

"Why did you drop the subject?"

She shrugged. "I thought you were a drifter and I . . . didn't want to pry."

"I have an ordinary family: three sisters, my parents, and a brother who is no longer living."

"Then why do I get the feeling there is something extraordinary about them?"

He felt as if an invisible fist had dealt him a swift blow. He'd never met a woman who was able to read his feelings about his family without being told about them in detail first. It shook him to have her guess so easily, and he began to talk about things he rarely discussed.

"When I was growing up, I had an ordinary family; my folks were farmers. Then when I was eighteen, my mom had a bad heart attack. A year later Dad was diagnosed as having a degenerative illness. I just took over. Someone had to. I saw to it that the bills were paid. I saw to it that my sisters and younger brother were educated, and that my folks had the proper nursing care. I built the farm into a ranch. In short, I assumed responsibility at an early age. While my friends were out growing up and kicking up their heels, I was working, caring for sick parents, and raising my sisters and my brother."

"Are your parents still living?" she asked, feeling a strange mixture of sympathy and awe, as she watched the play of candlelight on his tanned face.

"No. My brother isn't either," he said flatly. "He was killed a long time ago on a trip overseas. I'm not complaining. I'd do the same thing again, but

when my sisters were all grown, it became important to me to have some time to myself, to relax,
to enjoy life. Hell, I'm thirty-two. I've been tied
down a good part of my life. When I think about a
permanent commitment or marriage, I feel like
someone has dropped a noose around my neck
and is slowly pulling it tight."

His words generated an ache inside her, and
she reached over to squeeze his hand, seeing too
clearly the boy he must have been and the responsibilities that had turned him into a man too
early.

He squeezed her hand briefly and released it.
"I'm not trying to stir up sympathy. I would do
the same thing again as I said. No regrets over
that. But now I just have to take time for myself.
I've missed some things in life, and I'm old enough
to know I can't get the time back."

She hurt for him. He was matter-of-fact, and
she knew he didn't want pity, but she could see
too well what he had been through. She began to
understand better why he was so relaxed on the
Paradise. And she saw something else that increased a dull, throbbing pain in her heart. He
didn't want any type of lasting commitment.

As if he sensed the direction of her thoughts,
he said, "I'll be as honest with you as you have
been with me. I can't marry. I've been weighted
down with responsibility for a family that was like
a boulder chained to my ankles. I love them and I
took care of them, but I've had it with that kind of
life." His voice was gentle and patient, and he
sounded as unyielding as a concrete wall. "I won't
push you or rush you or coerce you, but I'd be

lying through my teeth if I told you I didn't want you in my bed."

Her heart thudded, and her breathing stopped for seconds. His words jolted her with the intensity of an electric shock. As he leaned closer, the flickering candlelight glowed on his prominent cheekbones and his Comanche heritage was suddenly evident. His voice was like silky fur, wrapping itself around her and heating her blood.

"I want you in my bed more than I've ever wanted any woman before. And I want you with me. I want you to ride with me at dawn, to see the ranch as I see it, to wade in the creek with me, to eat with me, to talk to me. I want you to smell the grass, watch the horses gallop, and sit in the shade of the cottonwoods with me."

She placed her fork on her plate and she could barely catch her breath enough to talk to him. Her voice came out as a whisper, and she felt as if she were drowning in a sea of blue as he watched her.

"I hate to waste a dinner, but I can't eat another bite," she whispered.

"I'll get the check from the waiter," he said gruffly, standing up and tossing down his napkin. He came around to pull out her chair. His hands drifted over her shoulders caressingly, and it took all the willpower she had to keep from turning and slipping her arms around his neck.

Jasmine was devastated by his words and his voice. He had spoken in level tones, but his words were so filled with emotion that she felt as if she were being torn in two. She wanted marriage, love, and commitment, the kind of life she had grown up knowing, the kind of love her parents shared. Long ago she thought she had found it, only to discover she had mistaken infatuation for lasting love. Now she was older and wiser and knew what she wanted. She knew she had found a man who was the most special person she had ever met—and he didn't want the same things she did at all!

She looked up at him as she stood. His eyes burned with desire. . . . If she hadn't known better she would have thought it was love. She wanted to throw her arms around him and tell him to try to forget the past, to try to love without fear of being bound and held by unwanted responsibilities. Instead she turned and walked quietly at his side, while she fought an inner quaking, because she knew in her heart that Matt Rome was unique.

He stepped away to summon the waiter and get the check, and she went outside into the chilly air to try to get her breath and bring a degree of sanity back into her life. Her world had spun out of its usual orbit into a new and startling path. She was at a loss, amazed at the feelings Matt stirred. She took deep breaths of the cold night air, looking at stars that twinkled overhead but were much less distinguishable than they had been off the coast of Bahía Grande.

"Jasmine," he said softly. She turned into his waiting arms, and he pulled her to him. He kissed her tenderly, a light, brief touch that quickly became passionate as raw emotions sought relief. His tongue thrust deeply into her mouth as if he had a desperate need to caress and hold her. He raised his head. "Come to the ranch with me. Come work for me."

All her life she had been practical and efficient,

and she was intelligent enough to know what a threat Matt Rome was to her peace of mind. A refusal was on the tip of her tongue. The sensible, safe course would be to say no, she realized.

"Jasmine?" he asked in a raspy whisper as he trailed his knuckles lightly over her cheek. He stood waiting while her heart thudded and her thoughts churned. Her throat burned, and the tears she blinked back stung her eyes, because she knew she was headed for heartache. But she tightened her arms around his neck and threw reason and practicality to the wind.

"Yes, I will."

His breath came out in a sigh of satisfaction before his lips found hers and he kissed her. He slipped his hands beneath her coat. For one blind second she wondered frantically what she had agreed to do, then she closed the door on doubt and yielded to the sensations that were storming her. His hands played over her back not so much in a caress, but more as if he were reassuring himself that she was there in his arms.

"Matt, we're in the parking lot," she said, turning her head a fraction and sliding her hands around to push gently on his chest. He buried his face against her throat. His words were muffled, but she heard them.

"Lord, I'm glad you agreed!"

His statement was as devastating as his kisses, because the sincerity in his voice was unmistakable. And some tiny little hope that Matt might not be as irrevocably bound to his freedom as he thought flickered to life inside her. She ignored the fluttering of her heart as she smiled at him.

"How long are we going to stand out here?"

A car swung into the lot, its headlights sweeping over them, and Matt smiled at her in return, taking her hand. "I guess this is a good time to go. How soon can you start work?" he asked, as he helped her into his car.

"How soon do you want me?" she asked in return, as he turned the car into traffic.

"Tonight."

"I can't come tonight!" she laughed, shifting in the seat to face him. He reached over to pull her close, and she adjusted her seatbelt accordingly.

"Okay, how about tomorrow?"

"For someone who's so relaxed, you're getting a little brisk!" she said with amusement.

"Brisk, huh? I'm anxious, eager, on fire—"

"Matt!"

"I need to get back to the ranch and the plant. I won't be around all the time, because I do work and I do earn a living."

Her mind was racing with details, and she thought in silence for a moment. "My parents are really old-fashioned."

He glanced at her with arched brows, and she went on to explain. "I'd like you to meet them, because it's a little unusual to pack and move to my employer's home to work."

"I'd like to meet them," he said in a polite, level voice. "You can hardly commute," he added dryly.

"How far out of town is this ranch?"

This time he grinned. "I really wanted this date. I told you I lived in a little suburban area, but that wasn't exactly right."

"Oh, brother! Where do you live?"

"West Texas, a few hundred miles or so from here."

"You flew down here for our date!"

"It was nothing. I own an aircraft company and I fly all the time," He squeezed her hand. "Okay?"

"I'm thinking," she said, adjusting quickly to this latest bit of news. Excitement hummed in her like the motor of the car, and she had to control the urge to put her hand on his knee.

Neither one spoke for a while until she said, "I'd still like you to meet my parents, so could you come for dinner tomorrow night?"

"Why don't you let me take all of you to dinner?"

"Thanks, but no. I'd like to have you over."

"Fine," he said, giving her a squeeze. She wondered how long it would be before she could sit close to Matt and not have her pulse skip faster.

"Then the next morning, I can be ready to go," she said. "How's that?"

"Miss Efficiency. That's excellent!" He signaled and turned into a parking lot.

"Where are we?"

"A quiet little place where we can dance," he said, parking the car. They rode the elevator to the top floor of a tall building and emerged into a room with floor-to-ceiling windows that gave a view of the lights of Houston. A jazz combo played, and some people danced while others sat at tables covered in white linen, candles and flowers. Jasmine knew it was a private club, and if Matt was a member, it meant he must be in Houston often.

The music was slow and quiet, and he took her into his arms to dance. He danced gracefully, but the closeness of his body, his legs brushing against hers, was a sensuous play on her nerves that built fires in her soul.

Hours later he took her home and spent a long

time kissing her good night. She didn't invite him inside because it was after two in the morning, and she was struggling to cling to a remnant of wisdom.

The next day it seemed as if her feet didn't touch ground, yet she wouldn't stop and admit to herself what she felt for Matt. She cooked a special crab casserole, and made a tossed green salad, hot rolls, and steamed broccoli for dinner. Finally, she dressed in a simple rust-colored wool dress, fastened her hair behind her head in a chignon, and waited impatiently for Matt to come back into her life.

Five

Matt stood outside her door wearing a tan western suit and a dark tie, and looking very handsome.

"Sorry I'm early, but I couldn't wait."

"I'm ready."

"I knew you would be," he said, as he came inside and closed the door. "Are your parents here?"

"Not yet."

"Then I don't have to be on my good behavior yet," he said, as he pulled her to him and kissed her fervently. He leaned over so she had to cling to him while she returned his kiss. He smelled like wildflowers and woods. The material of his coat was soft beneath her fingers, but his muscles were hard and warm. She could feel his heart pound as violently as her own. The intense reaction they had to each other was a never-ending source of amazement to her—a reaction that seemed to bridge their differences. He paused to look down at her.

"I'm going to fall," she said.

"Not ever," he replied solemnly, melting her with his implied promise. His gaze returned to her mouth, and her lips tingled eagerly while she closed her eyes and pulled his head closer. Each time they kissed something seemed to explode within her like a volcanic eruption spilling hot lava.

Suddenly he swung her up and stepped back. Smoothing her collar, he studied her. "Your folks should arrive soon. I'd better calm my ruffled feathers."

She smiled at him, and brushed his lips lightly in a kiss, hearing his swift intake of breath. Trying to ignore her own response, she took his hand. "Come get a drink," she said, leading him to her small yellow-and-white kitchen. "I have dry white Spanish wine because that's what you had on the *Paradise*."

While he opened the bottle, she checked on the casserole. The doorbell rang and they went to greet her parents.

"Mom, Dad, this is Matt Rome. Matt, meet my mother, Lou Kirby, and my dad, Bart Kirby."

Matt squeezed Lou Kirby's hand when she offered it, and then turned to shake Bart Kirby's hand. Her father was inches shorter than Matt, and slightly bald, and the only resemblances to his daughter were his green eyes and his quick smile. Lou Kirby was slender, attractive, and as friendly as her husband. They chatted as they went to the living room to sit down. Matt served the Kirbys wine and Jasmine joined them after she checked on their dinner.

"We want to thank you for rescuing our daughter."

Matt made a polite response while he watched Jasmine cross her long, shapely legs. She picked up her wineglass to take a sip and looked over the rim and into his eyes. His muscles tightened. She winked, and it was all Matt could do to pay attention to the Kirbys.

"Jasmine has told us about your interesting background," Lou Kirby said.

"After seeing how efficient she was on my boat, I knew she was the one to tackle my family's old letters."

Jasmine wrinkled her nose at him as her father continued, "I'm interested in your family papers because we had a Texas relative who lived on the frontier before he went to fight for the Confederacy. He became what they called a galvanized soldier."

Matt had a difficult time taking his gaze from Jasmine, but he did. "I've heard of them. Confederate prisoners who were given a chance to join the Union and go west to fight Indians."

"He was sent north to fight the Sioux, and then he came back to Texas after a couple of years when the war was over."

During dinner Matt learned that Bart Kirby had a few old guns, and when he told the Kirbys he had an antique gun collection, Jasmine groaned.

"Mom and I might as well bow out now and go somewhere else so you two can talk. Dad loves old guns."

Matt grinned at her. "We'll wait and talk about it later."

"If I want to keep peace in the family, I'll have to agree with you," Bart said good-naturedly, smiling at his wife. "I understand you build and service aircraft."

"Yes, sir. The plant is in Amarillo. We have a light jet . . ." Matt talked about his plant and his planes and the market, and he ate all of his dinner, but most of his attention was on Jasmine. He wanted to be alone with her, and the realization that she was going back home with him the following day made him as excited as a child at Christmas. And he wouldn't look any closer at his feelings for her.

He left several hours after her parents. He ached with frustration as he climbed into his car, and he glimpsed himself in the mirror. His hair was tousled from Jasmine's fingers, his mouth was as red as hers, and he shook his head at himself. She was old-fashioned all right, and in many ways not his type. But he was happier with her, more excited and intrigued, than he had ever been with any other woman.

He thought again about when he heard her calls for help and he leaned over the edge of the *Paradise* to find her alone in a boat full of papers. He chuckled in the darkness and began to hum. She was going home with him! And he had told her honestly and frankly that he wanted her in his bed.

Thoughts of that kind just made him ache more, and he swore softly while he tried to get his mind back to the problems of the latest design he had been working on.

They left early the next morning. Matt piloted the plane, and Jasmine sat beside him. She looked down as they flew above the rolling Cross Timbers, a belt of brush and trees extending northward to the Oklahoma border. Matt sat quietly at the controls, his profile to her. She thought about his sisters. She didn't know what his relationship was with them now, if they were still close or not. He seemed happy and excited, emotions that matched her own, and she wondered if his happiness was stemming from the same cause as hers. She'd spend at least three months living at his home and working with him! Her pulse skipped merrily, and she had difficulty keeping a full-fledged smile off her face. She twisted to look below at the flat, treeless land patterned in large rectangles of brown and yellow where fields had been plowed or were covered with dried grass from the long winter. It was the first of March now; it would be well into summer before her job would be finished. The prospects of spending so much time alone with Matt dazzled her.

A gray ribbon of interstate highway trailed over the land below. They flew above the Cap Rock, the dark scar cut in the endless brown land, the escarpment that was the eastern boundary of the *Llano Estacado*, the Staked Plains or Great Plains that lay like a giant, golden cape spread endlessly through western Texas into New Mexico. Gleaming jewels of emerald, occasional patches of irrigated land planted with winter wheat, dotted the vast grassland where water was at a premium.

Jasmine watched mesquite and cactus whip past below as she wondered if she were speeding toward heartbreak. She refused to contemplate it. She wanted to be with Matt, and at the moment, that was all that mattered.

His hand wrapped around hers. "What's on your mind?"

"You."

He groaned. "You pick the damnedest times to tell me things."

"You asked," she said. Feeling compelled to touch him, she drew her fingertips over the back of his hand, and noted that his long fingers should have belonged to an artist or an actor. She gazed into his eyes and felt as if she had looked into molten steel. Desire burned hotly enough in his expression to singe her nerves. He was solemn, and she drew in her breath, feeling a swift, consuming reaction to his hungry gaze.

"We're going to have some cold, wet weather soon." He pointed to his right. "See the dark cloud bank off to the north?"

She looked at the gray-blue clouds in the distance. "It reminds me of being at sea. You'll never know how happy I was when I spotted the *Paradise*."

"All that joy diminished a bit when you came on board."

"I was just speechless. Will I meet any of your family?"

"You'll meet all of my family. My sisters are going to adore you," he said dryly, and her curiosity increased.

She looked out the airplane window and wondered about his ancestors, the Comanche woman who had dared to marry a white frontiersman, as well as the frontiersman who had fallen in love with a Comanche. Had Matt inherited a streak of tenacity and arrogance from his long-ago relatives, the tenacity that made him stubbornly persist in getting what he wanted, and the arrogance that made him do as he pleased? He was a more complicated person than she had realized before, a combination of contradictory elements. And all put together in the most charming manner! His shoulders, beneath a jeans jacket over a plaid wool shirt, were broad and powerful; and she remembered exactly how it felt to be held against his broad chest. She *had* to touch him again and reached across the narrow space to place her hand lightly on his knee. He breathed deeply and laced his fingers through hers briefly. "Here's home."

She looked down as they flew over a series of buildings, corrals, barns, and dirt roads that cut narrow brown swaths in the pattern below. The long ranch house was a white frame structure, with a rail fence around the yard. The plane banked and then dropped down, skimming over a slowly turning windmill and a water tank. Matt set the plane down with ease on a short runway not far from the house.

He dropped lightly to the ground and swung Jasmine down. He wanted to pull her into his arms, but he knew his employees were there, so he slipped his arm around her waist and picked up the ridiculously small single suitcase she had brought. "If any one of my sisters was coming for even a week, we'd need the truck to get the suitcases from the plane to the house," he said, as he swung things into a waiting Jeep vehicle. He drove up in front of a four-car garage and when he stepped out of the Jeep, a furry dog dashed out and jumped against him.

"Hey! Wolf! Down, boy." He scratched the dog's

ears as Jasmine climbed out of the car. "Meet Wolf."

The dog turned, and wagged his tail as she reached out to pet him. "He's beautiful," she said, looking at his silver-tipped black fur.

"He's part collie, part wolf. And in spite of his greeting, he's a damned good watchdog. He'll be here with you when I'm out."

"Who feeds him when you're gone?"

"My housekeeper, Leah Amstead. She lives in that house," he said and pointed down the road. "She's here. I'll introduce you to her."

"Wolf's mighty friendly," Jasmine said.

"That's because you're with me. He knows you're accepted here."

"I'm glad of that," she said, and winked at Matt.

He picked up her suitcase and they went inside into an oak-paneled kitchen full of gleaming appliances. Matt introduced Jasmine to Leah, his short, plump, bespectacled housekeeper, before he led the way to a bedroom that used to belong to his youngest sister to deposit her suitcase. He watched her, aching to hold her, as she looked at the sunny, pale yellow bedroom, with white French provincial furniture. She smiled and remarked that the room was lovely after only looking at it for about two seconds. Then she turned to look expectantly at him, and his pulse jumped. He pulled her to him and kissed her long and passionately.

Finally she tapped his chest with her finger and gazed at him solemnly. "My dear Mr. Allnutt, this is a business arrangement, and if you kiss me too often, I won't get any work done."

"You'll manage, Miss Efficiency," he teased

mildly, forcing himself to take her arm. "Come see the house."

He showed her through his home, knowing she was right. He would have to go to work and leave her alone, or he wouldn't be able to keep his hands off her. "Here's my room," he said, watching her again.

Jasmine gazed at the spacious light-filled bedroom which was almost as large as her entire apartment—and was totally different from the disorderly stateroom on the *Paradise*. The king-sized bed was covered in a blue quilted spread, the carpet was a deeper blue, the walls were in a paneled dark wood, and there were floor-to-ceiling French doors that opened onto a patio. He had a fireplace, a wide-screen television, a broad oak desk and small file cabinet, bookshelves, closets, and a huge built-in gun rack. The individual touches were what she noticed the most: the seashells, the oil paintings of wild game—one of a tiger, another of an elephant—and a watercolor of a ship in full sail.

"How can you go from this to total chaos on the *Paradise*?"

He gave her a lazy, sheepish grin. "The *Paradise* is where I let go and relax completely."

"You have to work with the lines and the sails and the wheel constantly. If you really want to let go, why don't you go on a cruise—" She bit off her words, and his grin widened.

"On a cruise ship? And relax?"

She laughed. "I guess not! Every female on board would be after you."

"Not with this face, but I can't imagine relaxing on one of those."

She walked over to examine a collection of family pictures on one wall. There was a picture of his parents with three little girls and two boys. Matt was gangly and his hair was down to the collar of his shirt. She felt his breath on her neck as he said, "Mom gave us haircuts. That's why I looked as woolly as Wolf until I was thirteen years old." He pointed to two blond girls. "That's Tonia, the next in age to me, then Marina." His finger moved to a dark-haired little girl. "Vicki's the youngest. And this is Teddy, my younger brother." He pointed to another picture and she looked at a boy of about fifteen who had blond hair like Matt's, but a rounder face and wide blue eyes. He was in a football uniform and was smiling at the camera. Matt took her arm. "C'mon, I'll show you the other rooms."

They walked through the bedrooms, the dining room, and finally a large family room with braided rugs, a fireplace, western paintings on the paneled walls, and comfortable deep blue leather furniture.

The first sister arrived an hour after lunch.

Wearing a green sweater and jeans, Tonia was tall, slender, and as golden-haired as her brother. She had the same blue eyes as Matt, and Jasmine liked her immediately. While he scratched Wolf's ears, Matt watched them with amusement. He tried to tolerate his sisters' concern over his bachelorhood as long as it didn't interfere in his life. Long ago he had squelched their efforts at matchmaking. Now all he had to put up with was their not-very-subtle inspection of each woman he became seriously involved with. He had had a feeling they would adore Jasmine, and within the first half hour he knew he was right. Tonia invited Jasmine to lunch with her other two sisters, telling her she would call back to set a date. It was a brisk day, so Matt had built a fire, and all three drank hot coffee as they talked.

"You're one up on us—none of us has ever been on the *Paradise*," Tonia confided.

"It was absolutely unforgettable," Jasmine said pleasantly, and Matt grinned.

"Weren't you terrified to be alone in a rainstorm at night on the ocean? And even more terrified when you drifted away from your friends? I would have had screaming hysterics."

"Jasmine didn't have that reaction until she saw the *Paradise*," Matt said. Tonia laughed.

"I didn't!" Jasmine answered lightly, watching Matt's eyes sparkle.

They were interrupted by the ringing of the phone, and in a moment Leah appeared to tell Matt it was for him. For a few seconds after he had gone, there was silence, then Tonia set aside her coffee cup and ran her hand through the thick curls that made a cap around her head. "Has Matt told you much about himself?"

"He didn't at first," Jasmine admitted. "I thought he was a boat bum, and he let me go right on thinking it. I didn't know any differently until he appeared on my doorstep in Houston."

Tonia smiled, but there was more worry in her expression than joy. "Did he tell you about our parents' illnesses?" When Jasmine nodded, Tonia added, "And raising us?"

"Yes, he did."

Tonia sipped coffee and stared at the fire a moment, biting her lower lip, and suddenly Jasmine knew something about Matt was bothering Tonia. Something Jasmine didn't know.

"It was a little difficult to reconcile the Matt Rome I met on the *Paradise* to the one I met in Houston."

"My brother is a complicated man." There was another period of silence, then Tonia said, "I'm so glad you're here. We'll have a party so you can meet some family friends."

"That's nice, Tonia, but it's a little unusual," Jasmine said with amusement, wondering if his other secretaries had been introduced to family friends. "After all, I'm only a secretary and friend."

"You're more than that, I hope," Tonia said so solemnly that Jasmine caught her breath. And she realized that Matt was not the person she had first thought he was—and he might not even be who she thought he was after their second meeting in Houston, or his sister wouldn't be making such oblique statements.

At that moment he came back into the room with Wolf at his heels. A frown creased his brow, but as his blue-eyed gaze sought out Jasmine, his frown vanished. He sank down on a chair near her, stretching out his long legs. The three of them talked and had another cup of coffee, and finally Tonia said good-bye.

As soon as Matt returned from seeing his sister to the door, he crossed the room without slowing his step and took Jasmine in his arms.

"I want to show you some of the ranch. Want to go for a ride now?"

"Sure."

"Rather go by plane, Jeep, or horse?"

"You name it."

"Horse. Know anything about horses?"

"They have four legs."

"Okay," he said cheerfully. "There's nothing to it. I'll get you a gentle mount."

"You be sure you do. I won't be efficient if I'm in a cast up to my chin."

"I've got a real baby doll for you to ride. Her name's Pepper."

"Pepper? A baby doll?"

He laughed and gave her a squeeze. "She should have been named Sugar. Get a jacket and meet me in the kitchen."

"Sure."

"Jasmine—"

She turned to look at him. "It's good to have you here."

She winked at him and went to her room to get her jacket, but a silent song was running through her mind. She was happy, gloriously and ridiculously happy to be with him. He was the sunshine in her world.

A few minutes later she was riding beside him, across land that spread forever ahead of them in an endless vista of mesquite and brush. The only sound was the steady clop of horses' hooves on the dusty earth. The grass was dried and yellowed from the winter, and no signs of spring were visible yet. She shook her head, feeling the wind blow through her long hair as she thought about how the land gave a sense of freedom and permanence to a person's life.

"Why do you have to get away from this to relax?" she asked, mystified because the open space was one of the most serene places she had ever seen.

"To escape the phone for one thing. The call I just had may mean I'll have to leave soon. Do you mind working here alone?"

She shook her head, thinking she could stay there forever and be content. "It's lovely here," she said, breathing deeply and letting her gaze drift over the terrain. "I'd think this would relax you enough in spite of the phone. Just to come out here and ride in solitude—" She was ready to ask him if he preferred her to keep quiet while they rode, but her words died in her throat when her gaze met his.

He looked at her as if he hadn't seen a woman in ten years. Without a word he swung down off his horse and lifted her down from hers, letting her slide along the length of his body. Her hands rested on his shoulders and she slid down slowly until he held her so she looked directly into his eyes. Through the denim and wool of their clothing she could feel the strength in his arms as he held her.

"I want you," he said hoarsely, and she thought her heart would burst. She twined her arms around him and bent her head to kiss him.

She felt the tension in the coiled muscles of his body, and in his tight voice. On this remote ranch where it seemed to her he should be completely relaxed, he was as taut as a steel cable. Jasmine remembered his sister's remarks, and knew something was wrong. There was another side to Matthew Rome—a dark side she hadn't seen. She clung to him and kissed him with a bit of desperation, wanting what they had found together to develop and last.

As he released her, he said, "I knew you'd like it

here." His voice was tight, making it clear that it had been important to him that she like the ranch. She ran her fingers through soft locks of his golden hair that had fallen over his forehead, and it was on the tip of her tongue to tell him she liked the ranch because it was part of his life.

They mounted their horses and rode in silence. Matt moved ahead to lead the way, and she wondered if he wanted to be alone with his thoughts.

After dinner, they sat in front of the fire and kissed, and to her relief, he was more relaxed, more the Matt she knew. But later, when she lay in bed with only a wall between them, she worried and wondered about the parts of his life she hadn't yet seen. Sleep was impossible because she was too aware of Matt in the next room, and it was hours into the early morning before she relaxed and dozed.

The next day he took her to look at the plant. She walked beside him through the hangar, as he pointed out the latest design, their best-selling model. She had a brief look at the assembly line, then finally they went to Matt's large paneled office. He told his staff he didn't want to be disturbed, kicked the door closed, and pulled her down onto his lap to kiss her.

Finally, late that afternoon, they drove home to the ranch where he led her up to the attic. It was roughly finished in knotty pine and well-lighted.

As Matt stood in the center of a jumble of trunks and boxes, he waved his hand. "Here it is—all these boxes and that old trunk. I'll have a couple of the men move everything downstairs and we'll set you up in an office."

"You don't have to—"

"It won't be any trouble. I would have had it done already, but I didn't know far enough ahead of time."

"Let's take down a box now, so when I go to bed tonight, I can read."

When he didn't answer, she turned around to find him staring at her with his hands on his hips. She almost asked what was wrong, then she guessed it had something to do with her spending the evening reading in bed, and she bit back her questions.

They developed a routine. Matt wanted her to ride with him at dawn, then they ate breakfast together. He would go to town to the plant while she worked on the old letters. At night, they ate together and afterward, he would ask her what she had found in the papers that had been particularly interesting. She realized that Matt had read only a few letters, that for years he had put off sitting down and really going through the diaries and journals. Now that she was sorting it out for him, he was truly interested.

Every second she spent with him bound her more closely to him. Her first week at the ranch flew by. Tonia called and asked her to lunch on Wednesday, and Jasmine quickly agreed, eager to meet his other sisters.

Around midnight Monday a spring rainstorm came sweeping across the open land. The wind battered against the house, howling around corners. Jasmine lay in bed reading, her long black hair trailing down over her shoulders and onto her blue cotton gown. The lights blinked, thunder boomed, and she put down the book and sat up. She shivered and stared at the darkened windows, glad that Matt was home. Sleep was growing more impossible each night, because her interest was always more on Matt than on the papers or book in her lap. She stared at the windowpanes which were streaked with water, as lightning flashed, and thunder shook the glass.

Another bolt cracked, then thunder boomed with the sound of a gunshot, and the lights went off.

Six

She sat in the dark, not particularly alarmed, while memories of Matt's kisses crowded out worry about the storm. There was a light rap at the door, and it opened. Matt stood in the hallway holding a candle. He wore only his jeans, and the candlelight flickered over his features.

"Are you all—" His words ended when he looked at her.

Her gaze was drawn to his bare chest, his slender hips and tight jeans, then back to his face. The candle shed just enough light for them to see each other. She was caught in a hungry gaze that held hers like an iron band, a smoldering look that was an invisible caress on her raw nerves.

He came into the room without taking his gaze from her. With deliberation he picked up a glass coaster, tipped the candle to let the wax form a puddle, and set the candle in it so it would stand upright as he placed it on the table beside her bed.

Jasmine's mouth felt dry, and her heart thudded violently. She watched him, wanting to reach out and run her fingers across his solid chest. He sat down beside her, still holding her gaze with eyes that sent a clear message of his intentions. He reached out to catch a lock of her hair in his fingers, and flames built within her while he sat and did nothing more than toy with her hair. She couldn't get her breath. The flickering candlelight illuminated Matt's strong features, leaving the rest of the room in darkness. His gaze held hers, changing the tempo of her pulse and breathing, while he reached out to unbutton the neck of her gown.

Warm, callused fingers drifted over her bare skin, and she closed her eyes. "Matt . . ." His hand moved lower, in a feathery touch over her breast.

She gasped, her eyes opening as her hands reached for him. She wanted his arms around her, wanted his kisses. Her fingers moved over the tiny ridges of a scar, and as her lips brushed across his throat, she asked, "How did you get the scars?"

"In a plane crash."

It was one of his succinct answers, and at the moment, she didn't care to pursue the subject. His hands followed the curves of her body, moving down over her waist and her hips, then up again. "We have time," he said in a raspy voice, as both hands moved with deliberation along the sides of her breasts, stroking beneath their upthrusting fullness. His thumbs flicked briefly across peaks that had hardened with desire.

"Matt . . ." She pressed closer, locking her hands behind his neck as she looked into his eyes. He unbuttoned more of her gown and pushed it wide, freeing her breast and cupping the soft flesh in his big hand while he watched her.

Jasmine felt consumed by fire. She ached for him, but like the last pieces of a jigsaw puzzle falling into place and completing the picture, her last shred of resistance crumbled and she looked squarely at her feelings and knew she loved him with her whole heart. "I love you," she whispered, and watched as his eyes darkened. He tilted her face up to look at her searchingly.

"I ought to get up and walk out now, but I can't. I can't change what I am," he said solemnly, his voice tight with emotion. A vein stood out at his temple and a muscle worked in his jaw as she stared at him, understanding fully what he was saying to her. He wouldn't marry. There would be nothing permanent between them. She understood that he was battling his desire because he didn't want to hurt her. And if he didn't want to hurt her, he cared . . . Jasmine smiled and stroked his cheek.

"I know you have to have your freedom. I understand," she said, and raised her lips.

His breath went out in a long sigh as his arms tightened around her, and his mouth came down to open hers. His tongue was a fiery demand that she yielded to, and she was lost in swirling sensations. All barriers fell. She had admitted her love, and now she could touch him where she wanted to touch him, look at him without hesitancy.

He unfastened her gown and pushed it away, his eyes devouring her as he stood up to unbutton his jeans.

Matt's blood thundered through his veins, roaring in his ears while he watched her. Her eyes were emerald green and enormous, and her mouth was red from his kisses. Her cascade of midnight hair fell over her shoulders and breasts as he had imagined it so many times. He burned with eagerness, fighting to control desire until she was trembling and crying out for him. He wanted her more than he had wanted any other woman, more than he had known he could want someone. His only goal was to please her, to make her delirious with need, to touch and love her.

His hands shook as he tugged away his jeans, his eyes roaming lower to the beautiful pink and honey-colored flesh of her breasts. Then he looked at her eyes and found her staring at him as he stood nude beside the bed. He drew another sharp breath. With a groan he knelt on the bed and gently pushed her down.

Jasmine fell back, drowning in a flood of desire as Matt kissed her throat, his lips trailing lower. He rolled beside her, exploring with his hands, learning the texture and shape of her body and what stirred her to cry out eagerly, what made her gasp with pleasure. She kissed him with abandon, she caressed him, as need built within both of them. She was totally free and loving with him, trying to please him as much as he tried to please her.

The storm of passion carried them on an ever-rushing current until she tugged on him and whispered, "Matt, I want you."

He moved above her, pausing to drink in the sight of her, and she did the same to him, memorizing everything about his virile body.

He lowered himself between her thighs, and her slender legs held him. For a moment her body resisted, and in the back of Matt's thoughts he registered the fact that she hadn't been loved in a long time. He didn't want to hurt her, but when he slowed, her legs tightened and she pulled him closer. His heart thudded as he thrust into her waiting warmth.

Jasmine gasped, clinging to him while they moved to a stormy brink. His deep, steady thrusts were met by hers, as they reached a roaring peak that engulfed them. She cried out, clinging to him, feeling a union that was more than flesh joined with flesh, but was heart bound to heart.

"Jasmine, love," he said in a grating whisper as his long body shuddered with release. She had heard his words, and while her body responded with tremors of ecstasy, her heart locked away forever the whispered words, *Jasmine, love . . .*

He held her close, their bodies united while their hearts beat together. Jasmine stroked his broad shoulders and laced her fingers in his hair as he turned his head beside her. "I've wanted you since the first night on the *Paradise*."

She twisted to look at him. Perspiration dotted his brow and his eyes had darkened to a deeper blue. She rested her palm against his cheek, feeling the faint stubble, and she realized her lips were tender from scraping against his beard.

"I haven't ever known anyone like you," she said, marveling at the depth of her feelings for him. Something flickered in his eyes as if a shadow had passed across them. She felt a cool shiver of worry that was so brief, she just ignored it.

He buried his face against her throat, kissing her tenderly. His voice was muffled as he murmured, "I hope you can always accept me like you did on the *Paradise*."

She tightened her arms around him and closed out thoughts of tomorrow. He was in her arms and she loved him, and at the moment, that was enough. She kissed his temple and his cheek, and then he turned to kiss her deeply. It was a kiss that was filled not as much with passion as with affirmation. He raised his head and smiled at her.

"Thank heaven the lights went out. I've been praying for an excuse to come in here for nights now."

She laughed, feeling a giddy delight that made everything seem rosy. "The rain has stopped."

They both listened to the steady plop of water running off the roof, but the storm had passed.

"The rain served its purpose as far as I'm concerned," he said, propping himself on his elbow and shifting his weight to look at her. He stroked her smooth skin while he gazed at her rapturously. She was lovely, and so giving. Sensual beyond belief. His blood heated as he thought back on the past hour. He traced the lines where her deep tan stopped, such a contrast to the smooth pale skin that hadn't been exposed to direct sunlight. His heart began to pound as his body responded again to the sight of her. She was fantastic, gorgeous, sexy, and he couldn't remember feeling so intense an emotion ever before in his life.

Jasmine lay with her eyes half-closed, a faint smile on her face. Her thick black mane of hair was spread out behind her head, a few locks falling over one shoulder. She looked totally relaxed.

Her cheeks were pink, and her expression was satisfied, lazy, and languorous. She watched him, and he felt a silent rapport between them as if they were one in mind and soul. But at the moment they needed once more to be one in body.

He moved his hand lower, watching her draw a swift, sharp breath. Her eyes closed, and the smile vanished from her face as she reached for him. He sat up beside her, caressing her intimately, seeing how swiftly he could stir her. He tried to go slowly, tantalizing this time.

"Matt, come here. Come to me," she whispered, and pulled on his arm. He couldn't answer or talk. His throat felt tight as if his windpipe were constricted. He breathed deeply through his mouth while he stroked her, watching her hips writhe and seeing her yield to sensation.

Matt burned with need, but he waited, arousing her to another height until he couldn't hold off any longer and pushed her down on the bed to take her swiftly.

They didn't sleep until nearly dawn, and then Matt pulled her into his arms to kiss her awake. He nuzzled her neck. "I'm canceling everything at the office today and giving Leah a holiday. And I'll cancel your lunch with my sisters."

"You can't do that!"

His blue eyes glittered with determination while a lazy, taunting smile crooked his mouth. "Want to make a bet?"

Her voice lowered a notch as she twisted back on the pillow to look at him better. "Sure, you name the prize."

He kissed her long and deeply, then paused. "If

I cancel everything and give Leah the day off, I win you in my bed tonight."

"And if you don't, I win . . . What do I win, Matt?"

"What do you want to win?" he asked, and she felt a current of excitement run like lightning through her body. She pulled him closer. "I like the prize. I win the same thing."

That was the end of conversation for over an hour until he groaned and rolled off the bed. "I have to make a phone call and to do so, I have to go where I can't see you or touch you."

"Is that right?"

He stopped and turned. His body was radiant, his muscles developed and powerful, his skin tanned and taut. The sight of his manhood caused her skin to heat. He swore softly and left the room in a hurry, while she laughed, feeling excited and wildly in love. In love in a way she had never known. She stared at the open, empty door, and suddenly had a forlorn, stabbing wish that it could be forever.

Instantly, like slamming the lid on Pandora's box, she shut off thoughts of the future. Euphoria returned, and she slid lower in bed, thinking back over the night and morning, remembering Matt, knowing she loved him wholly and for always.

In less than twenty minutes he reappeared. He had just come from a shower, and again was dressed only in jeans. He walked straight to the bed and gathered her into his arms. "I win."

Her heart jumped with excitement and she stroked his shoulders. "What a sacrifice!" she whispered, teasing him.

"Yeah, I can tell," he said as he pushed away the sheet to kiss her breast.

She closed her eyes and lay back, moving her hands over him, giving herself up to his loving.

Abruptly he stopped, and she opened her eyes to find him moving away. "The house is locked up. We're alone. I'm going to cook breakfast. I'll fix you chocolate milk and whatever else you want—and then we'll see what we'd like to do. How's that?"

"Sounds wonderful," she said, letting her gaze drift over his marvelous chest and down to the bulge in his jeans.

"Dammit, I'm hungry," he said, but his voice was mild, and he came back down to take her into his arms again.

She kissed his throat, her tongue teasing him lightly. "Go cook your old breakfast!"

"Yeah, in a minute," he said gruffly. He caressed her, and the teasing stopped as she tightened her arms around him and shifted her body against his.

They spent the day locked in the house, shut away from the world. Matt unplugged the phones, and she was lost in a wonderworld of discovery and love. That night they made love in his big bed and finally slept locked in each other's arms. The next morning when they rode at dawn, she discovered he had taken three days off to be alone with her.

She called Tonia, and they made plans for lunch on Wednesday of the following week. While they talked, Tonia invited Jasmine to a dinner party at her house on Saturday night, the twelfth of April.

For the rest of the week, after she fell back into

a routine, Jasmine drifted in a rosy daze. She rode with Matt at dawn and breakfasted with him every day. It was the last week of March and the first faint signs of spring were beginning to show. She felt like singing all the time, and she was aware that Matt was coming home hours early from the plant, that no one disturbed them in the evenings, and that Leah was gone within an hour after dinner.

Matt flew her home to Houston on the weekend, and they spent Friday evening with her parents. Saturday morning he told her he had a surprise, and drove her to Galveston. As the black Lincoln sedan sped along the highway, Jasmine rode in serene contentment, alternately enjoying the view outside the car and the view inside. Matt wore tight jeans and a green knit shirt that revealed every rippling muscle. She had braided her hair and wore jeans and her red sweater.

She wanted to purr with happiness, and turned to look outside at the glorious day—or so it seemed when Matt was by her side. The sky was blue with fluffy white clouds building on the horizon. Sunshine sparkled like splashes of silver on the water as they crossed the causeway and came down into town, passing a bustling shopping center and a boulevard lined with oleanders and palms. He turned north toward the docks. When they reached the dock area, he parked the car.

"The *Paradise* is here!"

"I thought you'd like to see her again."

A snappy wind came off the gray-green water, as Jasmine stopped abruptly on the pier to stare at the boat. Her eyes widened in surprise.

Seven

Waiting like a lady bedecked for a party, the *Paradise* bobbed in its slip. Her deck was clean and scrubbed, and every line was neatly coiled or secured. Sunlight glinted on shiny ports, and the sparkling white paint on the hull looked new. Jasmine turned to look at him questioningly.

"I had it cleaned for you."

She stared at the cutter wordlessly again, then turned to take Matt's arm and march purposefully on board, and down into the galley where they could be alone.

"I didn't ask you to change!" she snapped.

"The hell you didn't!" he said, unable to keep from grinning. "My best intentions with you always get me into hot water. You tried your damnedest when you were on board to get me to do this. Women!" He threw up his hands and laughed.

"I tried for a few hours," she said. A mixture of pleasure, dismay, and regret warred inside her.

He shook his head and picked up his battered

gray cap from the counter, polishing the plastic penguin with his finger. He started to break the dangling string, and she caught his hand to stop him, placing the cap squarely on his head so that the string hung over his ear.

"I even got used to the string." She placed her arms around his neck and moved her body sinuously against him. "I like you the way you are, and I got used to the *Paradise*. And I understood the reasons you gave me for the disorder. It was quaint. Besides, now I know you work sometimes— you're not sloppy at the ranch. The *Paradise* is you."

His smile vanished, and his voice became husky while he slipped his arms around her waist. "I'll never understand you. I thought you'd be delighted."

"I would have been, if I hadn't gotten to know you better. Whatever you do is fine. You don't have to change."

"Lordy, how I pray you'll always feel that way!" he said vehemently, before his lips touched hers. Moments later he swung her into his arms, and she forgot the intensity of emotion in his voice that she heard in his last remark. "Let me show you my cabin."

An hour later he raised up over her. His brows arched and he asked, "*Quaint?*"

"What are you talking about?" she murmured, drawing her fingers over his chest. "You have such a super chest. You know that's the first thing I saw when you hauled me on board. And I couldn't talk for a whole minute."

"I wish I'd known that at the time," he said dryly.

"You did. You told me to look all I wanted, or something to that effect."

He grinned. "And now you've called the *Paradise* quaint. That's sort of like calling *me* quaint."

"You are," she said happily. "Quaint, sexy, adorable, sexy, oddball . . ."

"Stop there. I've gone from lazy and lecherous to adorable and sexy—a step up. If you'll roll out of this bed, I'll take you to dinner and then dancing in Houston."

"Sounds nice," she murmured, moving her bare hip against him. He groaned, pulling her into his arms. They didn't leave the *Paradise* until the next morning.

As they walked along the dock, Jasmine tugged on his arm and stopped him, looking at him earnestly. "I didn't want you to change the *Paradise* for me, but thanks."

He grinned and squeezed her. "I can put it back like it was in an hour. I've had it cleaned before." She turned to look at it and he watched her, tempted to scoop her up and carry her back to the cabin. Long strands of her silky hair fluttered in the wind, and her cheeks were pink from the fresh air. His heart beat a little faster as he studied her, and he ran his fingers through his hair distractedly while he faced the fact that he was in love.

She was lovely, fun, intelligent, giving, and so damned companionable. He hadn't thought it was possible to find in a woman what he had found in her. Yet, even as he acknowledged that he loved her, he stopped himself from thinking about their future.

Every time he started to feel strongly about a woman, he experienced a sense of being caged. But not now. It continued to amaze him that instead of feeling trapped or slowly suffocated, he didn't want to part from her even for a month. The knowledge shocked him. And he wondered how deeply he loved her. The emotions were new to him, unique, and disturbing. His mind went blank at the notion of commitment; he wasn't ready for a lasting relationship. Then why did something deep inside him hurt every time he thought about leaving her?

He took her arm. "C'mon, we'll talk in the car," he said solemnly.

The weather was balmy and sunny when they flew back to the ranch, and as Jasmine looked at the ground moving swiftly by below, she remembered her first flight north.

She looked at Matt's familiar profile, the green knit shirt that covered his broad chest, the flat plane of his belly, and his strong thighs. She knew what he looked like beneath the clothing, how it felt to touch and kiss him. She loved him more each day, and it made her want to be in his arms if only to look at him. She was deeply in love with him—at the moment life was perfect, and there was only the tiniest cloud on the horizon: tomorrow. She wanted marriage, but she still refused to think beyond the present. With a smile she reached over to place her hand on his knee.

• • •

Wednesday, the second of April, Matt came into the bedroom to wake Jasmine so she could ride with him. He was fully dressed in jeans and a sweat shirt. He had showered, and his hair was still damp on the ends. He looked happier than she had ever seen him, and she stretched out her arms to him.

He grinned and came down to crush her in his embrace. "I want to stay here all day, but I have appointments at the plant, and the first one's at nine o'clock."

"Such poor judgment," she said with laughter in her voice. "And I finally have lunch with your sisters today."

"Tonia liked you a lot," he said, leaning back to smooth her hair away from her face. "She's having a party for you a week from Saturday night, remember?"

"It's for you and your friends. She was nice and polite, but she was only here an hour. You don't know whether she liked me or not!" she exclaimed. Jasmine's whole world was rosy this morning. She couldn't stop smiling and she couldn't think of anything that could darken her day. Matt was handsome. The angular lines of his features were special to her now, his body devastating to her sight and senses.

"I came up to ask you to ride with me," he said. His smile vanished, and his voice became husky, as his gaze swept over her. He reached down to undo his belt buckle. "But now that I'm here and have seen you in bed, I have a better idea," he whispered, standing up to pull his shirt over his head. As he reached down to unfasten his jeans,

Jasmine slipped out of bed to wrap her arms around his neck and kiss him. With a muffled groan, he crushed her naked softness and warmth against him.

She closed her eyes blissfully, trembling with eagerness, her heart filled with love for him.

Several hours later she arrived at the restaurant in Amarillo where she was to meet his sisters. The restaurant lobby was filled with people, and music played softly in the background as Jasmine searched the crowd. She spotted Tonia's golden hair easily, and she made her way across the room to greet the others. Tonia began the introductions. "This is my sister Marina and my sister Vicki. Meet Jasmine Kirby—the woman Matt rescued and keeps hidden away at the ranch."

"Hi," Marina said, and Jasmine turned to face her. She was Tonia's look-alike in every way, except she was a few inches shorter. Marina had golden, curly hair, a ready smile, and deep blue eyes, and Jasmine could see a faint, feminine resemblance to Matt.

"I'm glad to meet you," Vicki said in a throaty voice. She had Matt's angular bone structure, the same prominent cheekbones, and a less arched bridge to her nose, but her face was striking and unforgettable. She was as tall as Jasmine, dark-skinned with black hair, and had the same deep blue eyes as the others. There was something different about Vicki. Where the other sisters were friendly, Jasmine sensed at once an icy reserve as she smiled at Vicki. Suddenly Jasmine wondered if lunch would be as simple and pleasant as she had expected.

"We want to hear all about your exciting rescue," Marina said, while Vicki fell in line behind the hostess, and they were shown to a linen-covered table in the corner near a wide window. Inside the restaurant the sounds of people talking were muted, and music played softly.

After they had ordered, Jasmine told them details about the fire and the explosion of the *Pelican* and how she was separated from the other members of the scientific team.

"Weren't you terrified floating around near the South Pole all alone?" Marina asked.

Jasmine laughed. "I was quite a distance from the South Pole, and yes, I was frightened. The *Paradise* was exactly what it's called—paradise. I was so glad to see a boat."

"What's it like?" Vicki asked with amusement, her cool blue eyes assessing Jasmine. Jasmine felt as if she was being scrutinized. Tonia and Marina had so openly welcomed her—Tonia had a party planned and had come out to the ranch the first day she was there to meet her. But Vicki was obviously holding back her approval until she knew Jasmine better. The three of them waited expectantly, and as Jasmine thought of Matt's need for privacy, she tried to choose her words with care.

"It's all Matt's. Haven't you ever seen it?"

"Never!" Marina said. "He says that boat is his own little world, and he doesn't want his sisters cluttering it. Sometimes I wonder if he knows we've grown up."

"We have bets on what it's like," Tonia said, as bowls of salad arrived for Vicki and Jasmine, along with a thick mesquite grilled chicken sandwich for Tonia, and enchiladas beneath golden, melted cheese for Marina.

Smoothing a napkin in her lap, Tonia continued, "I think it's a gorgeous yacht. Marina is willing to bet a lunch that it's a huge, deluxe houseboat with enough power to go wherever he wants."

Jasmine laughed, thinking of the *Paradise*, amused that Matt had kept his boat a secret from his sisters. "What are you betting on?" she asked Vicki, and again met a shuttered gaze that gave no indication of her feelings.

Vicki shrugged. "I think it's a sailboat, something that will keep him occupied while he's at sea. Something sleek and fast."

Two of the sisters looked at her expectantly while Vicki sipped hot coffee and took another bite of salad. Jasmine shook her head. "If you expect me to settle the bet, I'm going to disappoint you. I don't know much about boats. All I can tell you is the *Paradise* was the most beautiful sight I have ever seen."

"Is it a sailboat?"

"It has sails, it has a motor, and he lives on it. You'll have to view it yourselves to decide."

The sisters looked at each other, then Vicki looked at Jasmine, and this time there was a twinkle in her eyes.

"Whatever Matt has, he doesn't want us to know," Vicki said, "and you're not going to give away his secret."

All three of them looked at her, and they seemed

the most satisfied, pleased women Jasmine had faced in a long time. And she began to get mildly disturbed, because their joy was a little too obvious under the circumstances, and also a little extreme.

"What are our old family papers like?" Vicki asked.

"Very interesting," Jasmine said, admiring Vicki's simple navy woolen dress. "How come none of you has taken charge of them?"

"With Ginny, my two-year-old, I don't have the time," Tonia said.

"I don't either," Marina stated emphatically. "And I have twice as good an excuse—one four-year-old and one nineteen-month-old."

"And I haven't had time," Vicki said. "I'm in my second year with a law firm, and I work so many hours a week, I don't even keep count. The last thing that I'd consider fun would be reading stacks of old journals."

"Someday you all will read them, and you'll realize what a fine heritage you have. Do you have boys or girls?" she asked Marina.

"The four-year-old is Matthew, named for his uncle; the baby is Lisa. Right now Lisa is at Mother's Day Out, and Matthew is in preschool, so I have a few free hours."

Conversation shifted to children and then to Jasmine's background and her family, and during the course of the meal, Jasmine realized that all three sisters adored their older brother. She could understand why, but she was relieved to know they did.

Finally, after the sisters had paid the check,

tipped the waiter, and ordered final cups of coffee, Tonia said she had to go. Since Marina had come with her, both of them said farewell and left. And two minutes after they had gone, it occurred to Jasmine that they had planned it this way.

Vicki lingered, talking about Matt and their childhoods while the waiter refilled their coffee cups. "Has Matt told about raising us?"

"Yes, and about your parents' illnesses, how he got into the plane business, why he got the *Paradise*."

"You handled that tactfully—and you're so loyal to my brother. We really don't know any more than we did."

"I'm sure you could find out if you persisted."

For the first time Vicki smiled. "You're still not telling. I'm glad you're here."

"Thank you. It's nice to meet his family."

"I didn't mean here at lunch. You know, he laid down the law to us. We weren't to come out to the ranch during the past week."

"He told you to stay away?" Jasmine said, blushing deeply.

Vicki laughed. "He wanted you all to himself without us curiously prying and getting underfoot."

"I can't imagine you getting underfoot," Jasmine said frankly.

"I'm still the baby sister, but we get along pretty well. If I could visit, he wouldn't want to tell the others to stay away," she said gently, and Jasmine guessed there might be a closer bond between Vicki and Matt than between him and the others.

"Has Matt told you how he got so many scars?"

"He said he was in a plane crash."

Instantly Vicki's dark lashes fluttered down to hide her eyes, and suddenly Jasmine had a cold, prickly feeling that something was wrong.

Eight

Vicki ran her finger along the handle of the white coffee cup. "Ordinarily, I wouldn't go along with my sisters on talking to you like this." She raised her head and looked directly into Jasmine's eyes. "I'd say what my brother does is his business, how he handles his life is his own doing, but we all thought this time was an exception."

"I don't understand," Jasmine said, halfway tempted to tell Vicki to trust her first instincts and leave everything to Matt.

"We love our brother very much. He's been like a second father and mother to us, and we want him to be happy."

Jasmine waited in silence, because she felt they had gone beyond polite conversation.

"And you seem special to him."

"I'm not so sure about that," she said quietly.

"He's told us about you. That in itself is unusual. He told us about the children whom you send money to aid."

"It's not very much."

The other woman shrugged. "We could keep out of his life and leave you to discover everything about him just as other women in his life have." Vicki's expression changed. "I'm sorry. I made that sound as if there's been an army of women. There hasn't. I'm guessing he's told only two about his private life."

"He's thirty-two and very appealing. I know there have been other women."

"He'll tell you about how he got some of the scars in his own good time, but the news may come as a shock. I know it did to me. It won't be any less of a shock coming from us, but maybe you can handle it better with him if you have a little warning. Did he tell you he learned to fly when he was young?"

"Yes," Jasmine answered, a sense of growing panic in her voice. Something was terribly wrong for Matt's family to go through this painstaking effort to confide in her. The moment became suspended in time, etched in her mind. She heard the faint clink of dishes, the occasional laugh of a customer; she would remember forever how Vicki stared at her inscrutably, choosing her moment and her words carefully.

"He said your uncle had a small hangar where he serviced light aircraft," Jasmine said. "He said your uncle let people rent space, and later Matt went to work for him and built up the business."

Vicki smiled, yet there was a tinge of sadness in her expression. "He made it sound simple. My brother is what Tonia's husband, Russ, calls a fly-boy. He's wild about planes and flying. He expanded the farm into a ranch, then he struck oil.

All the time, he devoted every minute he could spare to flying. And when he inherited and developed the company, he bought out another aircraft company in Kansas and moved the whole thing to Amarillo. It didn't just build up gradually. The oil enabled him to go into the business in a big way—have you seen the Rome Aerospace plant?"

"Yes," Jasmine said quietly, a tight feeling building around her heart.

"Some of the planes are Matt's own design. He's had government contracts. He's done his own testing. He's been in more than one crash."

"How could you live through more than one!"

"He brought one plane down and got out of it before it burst into flames. One winter he crashed into a lake. Years ago he ripped a wing off, but still landed safely. He taught me to fly a long time ago, and I know the chances he takes, the stunts he likes to do."

Jasmine's chill deepened as she watched Vicki, who looked at her steadily while she talked, and suddenly Jasmine suspected Vicki wasn't finished. She acted like someone halfway through a story. She was still choosing her words carefully, and she'd paused to see if Jasmine had a comment.

"He'll tell you. If a woman stays with him long enough, he tells her. I don't know if my brother is the marrying kind. He hasn't been so far."

"I don't think he is yet," Jasmine said, her mind on all Vicki had told her.

They both sat in silence for a moment, then Vicki said, "You don't have anything to say. Would you rather have heard it from him?"

"No, I'm glad to know more about Matt. And I

didn't comment because I didn't think you were through."

Something flickered in Vicki's eyes, and she smiled briefly. "You guessed correctly. You're discerning. That's why we wanted to talk to you. You're different from the other women in his life. No one has been allowed on the *Paradise*. We can't even peek at it. We don't know where he docks it."

Jasmine laughed. "I only got to travel on board because he couldn't leave me to perish in the dinghy. Not because he wanted me there."

"He wouldn't have brought you to the ranch if he hadn't felt strongly about you. And from what I understood from Leo—a man who works for him—he could have gotten you in to Bahía Grande a few hours after he picked you up."

"That's right," Jasmine said, glad for some momentary relief from the somber conversation. "I didn't know it at the time."

"So my sisters and I have high hopes for you and our brother."

Jasmine sat quietly. If Vicki wanted an admission that Jasmine was in love with him, she would have to wait. It was too new a feeling for Jasmine to announce it to others.

"You said you didn't think I was through talking about my brother, and you're right. Matt has been getting government contracts for several years now. Have you seen a picture of our younger brother?"

"Yes, there are some at the house."

"I think Matt felt a sense of guilt when Teddy was killed. He was killed by terrorists when he was on a college trip in the Mideast."

"How terrible! I'm so sorry. I didn't know what happened to him."

"There wasn't any reason for Matt to feel guilty, but he was a parent to all of us, and I know that later he wondered if he should have let Teddy go abroad. But because of that, and because of the government contacts, and because of Matt's flying ability, he's involved in something else that he doesn't talk about and very rarely has told the women in his life about. But I suspect he'll tell you. He was tied in knots after Teddy's death, and some men in the government approached him about a secret mission to the Middle East to pick up a man and fly him out. The government didn't want to be officially involved. It meant landing on the desert and taking risks, and Matt was willing to do it."

For the first time Vicki faltered and paused. Jasmine felt cold, as if her blood had changed to ice. And all the little pieces of the puzzle fell into place, the little fragments of conversation she hadn't understood, and Matt's need for total relaxation.

"My brother has . . . sometimes I think he prefers life in the fast lane. You're not like the other women he's dated."

To Jasmine's amazement, Vicki's eyes filled with tears. She looked down and wiped them away swiftly, and when she raised her head, she was composed. "I love Matt; we all do. We want him to settle down and stop taking risks, because the odds aren't in his favor. There've been too many close calls, too many narrow escapes."

Jasmine was appalled to learn about Matt's life, and she was dumbfounded that the three sisters thought she could change him. "I haven't known him long," she said, and the words had a hollow ring as she remembered lying in his arms, the tender moments, the laughter, the companionable silences they'd had together. "I can't change him. No one can do that except Matt. He'd have to want to." Her voice was little more than a whisper, and Vicki looked so composed now that Jasmine thought maybe she had been mistaken about the tears.

"Sorry if I shocked you or made things difficult, but we thought if you knew, you could handle the situation better when he tells you."

"He might never tell me," Jasmine said, more to herself than Vicki, while she tried to grapple with the significance of what she had just learned.

"He will. He's never brought a woman to stay at the ranch house before."

"I'm working there."

"That's his excuse. Those papers have moldered in the attic for years. He could have hauled them down and given them to a secretary at the plant. And he's never allowed a woman—not a sister or a friend—on the *Paradise*. And Benny, one of the employees, told me you ride together at dawn."

Jasmine listened, amazed at how many of her activities had been reported to his sisters.

"My brother likes his solitude. If he shares it with you, he's found something special in you."

Jasmine wondered if that was true. She was at a loss for words.

"I hope we know each other long and well," Vicki said swiftly, as she stood up and moved away from the table. "I know you want to think about what I've said, so I'll say good-bye."

"Thanks again for lunch. Thank you for warning me," Jasmine said automatically, her mind barely on Vicki's departure.

Vicki nodded and said, "See you at Tonia's party. 'Bye."

Jasmine stared out the window at the traffic, hurting inside, because what Vicki had told her confirmed Matt's absolute statements that he wouldn't settle down, that he'd never marry.

She loved him totally . . . and she wanted to spend the rest of her life with him. Life without Matt was unthinkable, and yet he had warned her from the first that he wouldn't marry. And he was running such terrible risks. She closed her eyes as a shiver ran through her, and a sense of panic enveloped her. She had always wanted marriage and a home and family like she had known growing up. Now it seemed more of a remote possibility than ever.

She picked up her purse and walked mechanically out of the restaurant. The long drive back to the ranch gave her moments to think, but she wondered when or if Matt would tell her everything about his life. About an hour after she arrived back, she received a phone call from him.

"How was lunch?"

Her heart skipped as she listened to his deep voice, and she sank down in a chair, desperately wanting him to be home.

'Lunch was nice. Your sisters are consumed with curiosity about the *Paradise*. Now that it's clean, why don't you let them have a peek?"

"No way. They can get their own boats. Matter of fact, Tonia and Russ have one. So did you tell them in detail?"

"I left that up to you."

He chuckled. "You may have defeated half their purpose in inviting you to lunch."

"And the other half?" she asked, trying to keep her voice light.

"To get to know you. They're curious as cats about you."

"I'm not the first woman in your life, so I don't understand—are they always this way?"

"Always? You make me sound as if I've kept a harem! Honey," he said, and his voice changed, the amusement vanishing.

Honey. she closed her eyes and clutched the phone, aching to hold him. She wanted to lock him in her arms and keep him forever.

"I'm sorry," he continued, "but something's come up. I have to leave town. I should be back Friday."

Fear that he would be leaving the country flashed like lightning through her body, then reason replaced it swiftly. He couldn't go far in two days. Her disappointment that he was going at all was strong, because she felt an overwhelming need to be near him after learning so much about him.

"Are you coming home to pack?"

"No. I have to leave right away. I keep a few things at the office for emergencies like this. I'm flying to Washington, and I'll be at the Windsor Hotel. Here's the number."

She wrote the number down and read it back to him. "I'll miss you, but I guess I'll catch up on some of the work."

"I wish I could get home for an hour first," he said in a husky voice. "I'll call you tonight. Oh, Leah will be close if you need someone. You know the number of the bunkhouse. And Wolf is a good watchdog."

"I have yet to hear him bark, much less growl."

"He can. I'll miss you. 'Bye, Jasmine," he said, and then he hung up.

She replaced the receiver and stared at it, feeling separated from him by more than distance. He was so complicated. She sighed and went to the kitchen, where Leah was spreading tomato sauce over a meatloaf.

"Mr. Rome won't be home for dinner. He's leaving town for two days."

"He's been around longer than usual. I'll just put a small potato on for you."

"While he's gone, I can cook for myself, Leah. I don't mind at all. That's what I'm accustomed to doing."

"I'll cook, Ms. Kirby, because that's what I'm paid to do."

"For just me—you take a little time off. I don't eat much."

"Yes, ma'am."

"I'll be in my room if anyone calls."

"Yes, ma'am. Ms. Kirby—" She paused a moment and wiped her hands on a towel. "I'm glad you're here. Mr. Rome looks happier than I've ever seen him."

Jasmine gazed into the woman's hazel eyes and smiled. "Thank you, Leah. That's nice to know."

She went upstairs and sat down at her desk, picking up a yellowed journal to read.

Matt came in at six o'clock Friday evening. She heard the car coming up the road and went out the back door to wait for him. She smoothed her hands on her jeans. Her pale pink cotton blouse was open at the throat and her hair was looped and pinned on top of her head. Her pulse quickened as she watched him climb out of the car and slam the door.

His hair was tangled, his tie pulled off and sticking out of the pocket of his charcoal suit, the white shirt collar unbuttoned. He looked tired, rumpled, and marvelous! He carried a briefcase that he dropped when he met her. His arms wrapped around her, and he crushed her to him. His kiss ignited a raging fire that swept through her in a rush. She closed her eyes, holding him, kissing him back, her tongue thrusting deeply against his, as she tried in every physical way to affirm their love. He flung the briefcase through the open door, scooped her up and kissed her again, as he walked inside. There wasn't time for words; they both seemed to feel a desperate urgency. He kicked the door shut and turned to let her reach down and lock it.

"Leah?"

"She's gone. I cooked dinner. It'll keep," she whispered.

"It'll have to," he said, as his mouth covered hers again. He carried her to the living room where he swung her down on the sofa. Swiftly, he flung off his coat and pulled his shirt out of his trousers, then he came down to hold her and caress her, his hands seeking her breasts while she gasped and turned to him.

It was hours after dark before they ate dinner,

and by the time they did, she knew something was wrong. He was solemn, and slightly tense, and as she worked in the kitchen, she would turn and catch him staring at her speculatively.

After talking with his sisters she could guess why.

They cleaned up the kitchen together and as they started out of the room, he stopped abruptly. "I forgot. I brought you a present."

He ran out to the car and returned with a large box wrapped in blue paper and tied with blue ribbon.

"Ah," she said, trying to guess what it was while she carefully worked the ribbon loose. Matt lolled in a kitchen chair. The chair was tipped back, and he sat with one knee bent, his ankle resting on his other knee while he watched her.

"Holy Moses. We'll be here until tomorrow. Tear the paper off."

She wrinkled here nose at him. "It's my present. I want to keep the ribbon and the paper. They're special," she said with a smile, making him grin as he folded his arms across his chest.

She stood up to open the box, pulling out packing and another box from inside. She opened it and removed sheets of crisp, white tissue paper.

Nestled inside was a large chunk of crystal. At first glance it looked like a beautiful, oversized rock. She picked it up and watched it catch the light in its depths. Deep in the center a ship very similar in appearance to the *Paradise* was etched. She saw the card and recognized at once the name of a fine crystal maker.

"It's beautiful!" she exclaimed. "Thank you!"

"You're welcome," he said, looking pleased. She

put it down carefully and sat in his lap to kiss him.

After a few minutes they moved to the family room, sinking down on the sofa.

"How was Washington?" she asked, twining her fingers in his hair.

"Busy. How was the ranch?"

"Quiet."

"We have a party to go to tomorrow night at Tonia's."

"I know. I don't have to wonder what to wear—I only brought one dress."

"Well, hell, go into town and get another one if you want," he said, while he studied her as if seeing her for the first time.

"My dress is fine. It's just that you've seen it before."

His blue eyes were dark and opaque, and she could detect worry in his expression. The reassurance of the last few hours of their lovemaking and companionship diminished, and a lurking cold fear plagued her. She continued to twist short locks of his hair through her fingers. "I'm glad you're back."

"Did you discover any new facts about my ancestors while I was gone?"

"Yes, I did." She sat up, knowing now that he was postponing something, and that she had to let him talk in his own time. "Did you know you had a relative who was almost hanged for voting to stay with the Union and not secede?"

"In Texas?"

"Yes. They hanged his friend and intended to hang him, but they ran into a band of Kiowas. In the melee he escaped from both his fellow Texans and the Indians."

"We were a wily bunch," he said with a grin, toying with a long strand of her hair. "I have to go away again soon."

He said it quickly, flatly, watching her impassively, and her heart lurched.

Nine

"Where are you going?" she asked anxiously.

He drew a deep breath. "I have some business I need to take care of, and it means being out of town for a couple of weeks or so. Remember, when I told you about this job, I told you I might be gone some of the time."

"Do you want me to stay and work?" she asked. She hoped she had sounded normal, because inside she began to hurt, little splintering aches like the first faint cracks appearing on the smooth, frozen surface of a pond. "I can go home and come back later."

"I'd like you to stay." He stared at her solemnly. "If you go, you'll get another job."

He wasn't going to confide in her. If Vicki hadn't told her about Matt, she wouldn't have the slightest idea now that he was holding back telling her about himself. He had withdrawn, and she knew she had to smile and act as if she didn't know a thing had changed.

"Whatever you want," she said, determined to keep her voice light.

He smiled at her while he studied her features. She framed his cheeks in her hands, leaning closer. "I love you," she whispered bluntly, in all honesty. She tipped her head to kiss him, and her worries vanished.

Three hours later after they had made love, she lay in his arms in front of a dying fire, her lustrous mane of midnight-black hair spread over the golden mat of his chest curls. He said softly, "I'm leaving in a few days, on Monday. I'll be gone about a month."

Jasmine lay still. Suddenly all her senses were alert in a new way. She waited to see if he would elaborate.

"I can't talk freely about where I'm going or what I'm doing, but it's a voluntary mission. I'm flying into a dangerous foreign country to deliver some supplies."

She raised up, firelight bathing her with a golden reflection. "Do you have to go?"

"Yes, I do," he said, twining her hair around his fingers.

She drew her hand across his chest while she debated what to say, how much of her thoughts to reveal to him. "And you're sure you want me to stay and work while you're gone?"

"Yes, I'm sure," he said gruffly, his fingers moving to her shoulder to rub back and forth lightly. She lay back down and moved as close as possible to him, staring up at the ceiling. "I'll miss you terribly."

He rose this time, propping his head on his elbow, turning her to face him. "You knew this. You knew before I told you."

"Vicki told me about your missions," she admitted, wondering how on earth he had guessed that she already knew about his trips.

"I'll be damned!" he snapped. "My sisters—"

"Don't be angry. They like me and wanted to warn me about you. They thought I could handle the news better this way."

Speculation replaced anger in his expression. "Can you?"

"I think so. I'm trying. It's difficult to . . . think about your doing something so dangerous."

"It's something I want to do," he said firmly. He stared at her, bracing himself for the flood of protests he had gotten from his sisters and the two women to whom he had confided his plans in the past.

Jasmine smiled at him and pulled slightly on his shoulders. "Come back down here."

Surprised, he couldn't resist asking, "No protests?"

"What good would they do?" Jasmine asked with a lightness in her voice that she didn't feel. Too clearly she could hear his words that every time he began to fall in love, he felt as if someone were slipping a noose around his neck. Love wasn't a noose, and if she could do so, she'd let him go without a protest.

He settled beside her, and she sensed his heartfelt relief in the passion of his kisses.

Their approaching separation made their moments together more urgent. Matt was astounded that she would let him go. And he dreaded leaving—something that he had never experienced before. He had always felt it a thrill to fly into danger, and for a long time, he felt a sense of duty to prevent what had happened to Teddy from occurring to someone else. But now, as the hours ticked by, he felt only reluctance about the coming assignment. And another emotion overwhelmed him—he loved Jasmine enough for a permanent commitment. The future without her was impossible to consider. And he had known for a long time she was in love with him—he didn't think she would have given herself to him fully if she hadn't been.

The next morning after breakfast he took her arm and said, "Get your purse. I'd like you to go into town with me. I want to buy a new tie."

"Sure," Jasmine answered, surprised he'd want her to go along on such a simple errand, but glad to be with him.

She dressed in jeans and the red sweater, and they drove to town. It was the second week of April. The yellow leaves and grass were now changed to green. The early fruit trees were in bloom, and spring wildflowers brought yellow and blue splashes of color to the roadside. Their conversation was relaxed and normal until Matt parked the car and came around to open the door for her. His eyes twinkled with amusement. "First thing, I want to buy you a present."

"What's so funny?"

"I want to get you a dress for tonight and I know you're going to take my head off for making the offer."

Happiness tickled her as she watched him. "How could I get angry with you?" she teased. "It's a beautiful day, and I like being with you. Now forget the dress, and let's get you a tie."

"No." Matt watched her, bracing for what he knew was going to come. "I want you to wear something special tonight. I want to do this."

"You sound like my dad," she said, smoothing a lock of blond hair off his brow, curbing the impulse to let her fingers drift down his cheek. "I'll go get a dress, and surprise you."

"What I had in mind, your dad wouldn't select. Come on, Jasmine, humor me."

"This is ridiculous! Here we are arguing over the silliest thing. I'll go get a new dress, then we'll both have what we want. It's the end result that counts."

"Not at all. Not ever. You of all people . . . to say the end result counts!" he persisted, watching her and hoping he could talk her into what he wanted.

"Matt, people are staring."

"I don't blame them. I'd stare too at a sexy woman arguing with a guy about buying her a present. Don't be such an independent woman. Humor me." He raised his voice and let his drawl become more pronounced, "Darlin', you have only one dress. Let me buy you another one."

"Matt!" she exclaimed, laughing.

"C'mon, humor a quaint guy," he said softly, wanting her to yield, feeling a mounting excitement as he thought about the evening ahead. At the moment he wanted to give her the world. He loved to watch her laugh. He was on fire when her green eyes darkened with desire, and now he was having difficulty keeping his hands away from her.

She threw up her hands. "I surrender. Whatever you want, but you have an unscrupulous side to your personality."

"When it comes to getting what I want, I suppose I do," he said cheerfully, as he took her arm.

He took her to a small shop where they were served coffee while dresses were brought out for Jasmine to view. She selected one black and one red silk and left to try them on.

Matt waited, his long legs crossed, thoughts of the weeks ahead crowding him. He should pay her for her work, send her back to Houston, and let her get another job while he was gone, but he couldn't bear to think about her away from the ranch. And the prospect of her dating someone else was unthinkable.

She stepped out from behind the curtain, and he felt a tightness in his groin as he watched her walk toward him. She had a graceful, sensual way of walking that she seemed totally unaware of, a way of moving with the slightest sway to her hips, which he had memorized.

The black dress was simple, with long sleeves, a high neck, and a flared skirt that swirled around her legs. Matt viewed it with interest as she twirled in front of him. She was beautiful, and just the sight of her sent his pulse racing.

"It's nice," he said, thinking that was the understatement of the month. The dress was gorgeous on her, and he wanted to unfasten every little button down the back of it.

"I'll try on the other one," she said and disappeared, leaving him alone with his thoughts. He'd be gone a month, and he would be in danger. Only twice had he confided in the women he dated about his missions, and both times it had ruined the relationship. Yet so far, Jasmine seemed to take everything in stride just as she had done on the *Paradise.* He grinned as he thought about the bill on his desk for the cleaning and repair job to the *Paradise,* and it had only aggravated her.

A month away from her. He shifted in the chair. It hurt to think about being separated from her. His brows drew together. He couldn't remember ever feeling this way before. Jasmine was special. At the damnedest moments, his mind would drift and he would think about her laughter or her kisses or some fragment of their conversation. He distractedly ran his fingers through his hair. He loved her. And he was constantly, deeply relieved about the way she had accepted the news of his trip. As he was mulling over his feelings, Jasmine reappeared.

The impact of the sight of her took his breath away. The dress was a flame that licked at his senses as she moved. The scarlet silk was supple and clinging, hugging each curve of her body. The dress had the same simple lines as the black one, except that it had a narrow skirt, a V neck, and short sleeves. And the moment he saw her in it, he knew which dress he preferred.

Her hair was slightly tousled from trying on the dresses. Wispy locks trailed down over her ears and neck, making her look more vulnerable and touchable. His blood heated when he thought about taking her home after the party.

"I like that," he said in a deep voice, as he looked into her eyes. Her dark lashes fluttered, and she placed her hands on her hips, turning for him to view the back of the dress which had a zipper that ran from the nape of her neck to her buttocks.

"Want to see any others?" he asked in the same husky voice, while he mentally peeled away the vivid silk.

She shook her head. "I think you like this one," she said, her eyes wide open. The pink tip of her tongue moved across her lower lip the same way it did in moments of deepest passion, and Matt was on fire.

"That's right, I do like it best," he said roughly, standing up, trying to get his mind elsewhere to calm his senses.

Matt paid for the dress, then took her to a department store, gave her use of his charge card, and told her to get what she wanted to wear with it. He knew she wouldn't use the card, but he didn't want to trail around the store with her.

When she returned, he took her packages to the car and drove to a jewelry store.

"What about your tie?"

"I decided to wear an old one."

"Matt! That was just an ex—"

He leaned across the seat to kiss her, knowing it would end the conversation. When he moved back, she gave him an exasperated stare. "Why are we in front of a jewelry store?"

He bit back a smile. "I want to get you some kind of simple necklace and bracelet to wear with the red dress. Let me do as I please, and don't make a federal case out of it."

"Sure thing, dearie. You're a little daft."

"That goes with being lazy and lecherous."

She selected two thin gold chains and a bracelet to match, and Matt felt satisfied when he saw how pleased she was. She chose to wear the bracelet home in the car, and she couldn't stop admiring it. "This is lovely."

"It sure as hell is!" he said in a raspy voice, leaning across the seat to kiss her again, tasting her sweetness, the softness that he needed so badly.

He stopped at the plant for half an hour, then they made the hour's drive home and he left her alone because he had some phone calls to make and some paperwork to do. He sat closed in his office, his feet on the desk, a notepad and an open ledger in front of him, but his mind was on Jasmine. She was like the air around him, necessary, vital, constant. He couldn't imagine telling her where he was going or what he was going to do, yet they had been so open with each other until now.

He was still shocked at the intensity of his feelings for her. It was something new to wonder about, to examine, this fluttery feeling inside him when she smiled or came into a room, the hot spasm of desire she could evoke merely by crossing her legs. Her whispered words and companionable silences were as important as the moments of passion they shared, but the memory of holding her in his arms, of her softness beneath him, encompassing him, set his pulse hammering.

It was a new development in his life at a time when he hadn't expected one, a development he would have thought impossible a month ago. He rubbed the back of his neck, recalling how he looked down at the dinghy and saw a beautiful woman with a boat full of papers. He laughed as he dropped his feet to the floor and stood up, throwing down his pencil. Outside the spring landscape beckoned him temptingly, and he took a deep breath, feeling restless and full of energy. He decided to get ready for Tonia's party, because he wasn't getting any work done.

Jasmine's bedroom door was closed and a swift image of her bathing came to his mind. With an abrupt change of direction, he turned and knocked on her door.

"Come in, of course," she shouted, and he grinned.

"It's about time to get ready to go to the party. I thought maybe you'd need some help."

"Help?" she asked. She stood in the doorway of her bathroom, a towel wrapped around her body, droplets of water glistening on her smooth, tanned shoulders. Her sleek black hair was wet, plastered to her head, making her eyes look larger than ever.

He crossed the room to take her into his arms, and his worries about leaving her soon melted like snow in the sunshine.

"You're going to get wet."

"You don't say," he murmured, crushing her to him, not caring whether he fell in the tub.

Later he waited downstairs for her until he heard her bedroom door open. He walked to the foot of the stairs, his pulse jumping at the sight of her.

She was dressed in the scarlet silk, but now her hair had been neatly combed and pinned up. She wore matching red shoes which she must have purchased at the department store. They had absurdly high heels, but the height added to the graceful, long line of her legs. Tiny diamond earrings twinkled in her earlobes, and the thin gold chains caught glints of light, but it was Jasmine who took his attention. The dress clung, the soft fabric shifting with each sinuous movement of her hips and legs. Her shapely curves were clearly revealed, and as he stared at her he could see her body react. The twin peaks of her breasts hardened, thrusting against the thin scarlet material.

His body had its own reaction and he walked away, trying to calm down. When he faced her, she looked at him with unmistakable love in her eyes.

"I would sure as hell rather stay home!" he said roughly.

"So would I, but we can't. Tonia has planned this party since I first arrived."

"I know that. My sisters! They are a meddlesome bunch."

"That's because they love you," she said, taking his arm, feeling the hard muscles beneath his dark coat.

He groaned. "This is hell. I want to crush you in my arms . . ."

"And wrinkle my dress, and tangle my hair, and I'd have to start getting ready all over," she said breathlessly, knowing that's what he would do when they came home.

"C'mon. Let's get this over with."

"Yes, dear Mr. Allnutt. You sound like a growly bear." She laughed lightly, a giddy happiness swirling around her as she hurried to the car with him.

He drove fast, the powerful car eating up the wide open road. A full moon bathed the flat prairie in silver light, giving it a lustrous glow that couldn't begin to match the one Jasmine felt inside.

Tonia's two-story colonial house was ablaze with lights, and inside a man played the piano quietly while guests mingled. Tonia appeared in a swirling yellow chiffon dress that complimented her golden hair and fair skin.

"Here you are! My guest of honor. Come meet everyone, but first meet my husband Russ."

Jasmine said hello to a tall man with warm blue eyes, a firm handshake, and a thatch of hair as yellow as his wife's. "I'm glad to meet you, since I've been hearing about you for weeks now," Russ Fleming said.

"There's nothing to hear."

"You came floating up in a dinghy adrift alone on the Atlantic—" He glanced at Matt. "That's nothing?" They shook hands. "It's good to see you, Matt. Didn't you think you were seeing things?"

"I will never as long as I live forget that moment," Matt said solemnly, looking down at Jasmine. She winked at him, and he slipped his arm around her waist.

"No, you don't!" Tonia said, taking Jasmine's arm and pulling her out of Matt's grasp. "Matt can monopolize you later."

As Jasmine walked away, she heard Matt say, "I was asleep when I heard someone crying, 'Help . . .'"

His voice trailed off, and then she was busy with introductions and greetings. She saw Marina and met her husband, Drake Eden, a short, thin, sandy-haired man, who was as friendly as his wife. As she moved around the spacious living room decorated with dark wood furniture and a thick Persian carpet, she spotted Vicki, who looked beautiful in a simple black dress. They said hello briefly, but the crowd around them prevented conversation and then Vicki moved away with a man who leaned close to talk to her. As the clusters of people shifted, Matt and Jasmine were together again, and then parted.

During a dinner of thick, buttered steaks and cheese-covered potatoes, Jasmine sat across from Matt, and next to Drake and another man who was an old family friend. It was distracting to look into Matt's eyes, yet be with a crowd of people. Once, she had turned to talk with Drake about the local politics in Houston. While she listened to Drake, she glanced at Matt. He was watching her intently, his gaze lowered to her lips. She forgot what she had been about to say, then she realized the silence was too long, and she turned back to Drake. "I'm sorry. I forgot what I was about to say," she admitted bluntly.

"So I noticed," he said with a grin. He lowered his voice to whisper in her ear. "Maybe I should say, 'Welcome to the family.' "

She felt a blush creep into her cheeks as she looked up at him, and suddenly she was solemn. "I think that's a bit premature."

"I hope not," he said warmly, and she relaxed again and smiled at him.

After dinner as the guests mingled, she found herself alone with Vicki.

"That's a beautiful dress," Jasmine said, thinking how different Vicki was from her other sisters. She would have guessed Vicki was the oldest sister instead of the youngest.

Vicki smiled over her drink. "How are things?"

"He's told me he's leaving Monday for about a month."

"Oh?" Vicki said, her features impassive. "Are you going back to Houston?"

"No. He said he wanted me to stay and continue to work."

"I hope you do. We'll have to have lunch again. Call me when you're coming to town."

"Thanks, I'd like that." She glanced across the room at Matt. He stood with two men and three women, and his head was bent so he could hear something the woman next to him was saying. Her hand was on his arm and they laughed, looking into each other's eyes, and Jasmine felt a pang of despair. She was such a small part of his life. These were his friends, some he had known all his life, his family, probably past girl friends. His work, his social life and his family were separate from his relationship with her. All they had together were intimate moments of closeness that had been physical as well as emotional, a closeness of mind and spirit, yet she wondered how much that counted with him. To him it might just be a passing thing.

He turned his head, and his eyes met hers. A tingle stirred inside her in response to his gaze as she watched him, thinking he was the most appealing man she had ever known. And at the moment she wanted to be alone with him.

Without taking his gaze from hers, he said something to the others and moved away, heading in Jasmine's direction. Her heartbeat quickened as she continued to look into his eyes, captured now by his steady, blue stare. Then he was so close he was almost touching her. She stood by the wall, and his broad shoulders effectively blocked them off from the other guests.

"Ready to go home?" he said, running his finger lightly on her wrist.

"You know the answer to that," she said softly, wanting to reach up and push back a golden lock that curled on his forehead. "But it's too early to leave. I don't want to be rude."

"It isn't too early, and my sisters think you hung the moon."

"They don't!" she exclaimed, aware of his fingers drifting higher on her arm in a light touch.

"I think they hope you'll reform me."

"I'm trying," she said, feeling that current of excitement only Matt could stir so easily.

"Let me show you Tonia's utility room," he said, taking Jasmine's arm.

"Matt! Don't be ridiculous!" Laughter bubbled in her voice, while sparks danced in her veins like tiny flames. "You'll embarrass me!"

"Of course, I won't. You're far too poised to be embarrassed." He gave her a speculative look. "You seldom blush, but my brother-in-law caused you to at dinner."

"Nosy!" she quipped, not about to tell him Drake had welcomed her into the family.

"I'd be jealous if I didn't know what a sound marriage they have."

"He was talking to me about you, and I'm not going to say another word on the subject."

"And it made you blush? Now I am curious!" They went into the kitchen and he paused. "Ella, this is Miss Kirby. Ella is the one who keeps this household rolling along on an even keel."

"I'm glad to meet you," Jasmine said to a tall, thin woman dressed in a white uniform.

Ella smiled. "Glad to meet you. Nice to see you again, Mr. Rome. We've been wondering when you'd be over."

"Here I am. I'm showing the house to Miss Kirby."

"Go right ahead," Ella said, turning back to a tray of chocolate drops and bonbons.

Matt rounded a corner, flipped a light switch, and pulled Jasmine into a room filled with baskets of laundry, an ironing board, and a washer and dryer. He closed the door behind them.

"Matt, this is absurd and embarrassing. Ella will know we're in here!"

"So? Ella's old enough to understand human nature." His arms banded her waist as his jacket pushed open and he pulled her against his chest. "I can't wait another moment to hold you."

"If you kiss me, my makeup, my hair, and my dress will be awry—"

"Terrible thing for Miss Efficiency to be awry," he teased, a sparkle in his blue eyes. "Although I've always liked rye better than wheat or white or—"

"Will you stop?"

"Yeah," he said, sobering, his gaze hungry and determined as he lowered his head to place his mouth over hers.

His breath tasted of wine; his clothing smelled faintly of smoke, but his tongue drove away thought as he kissed her deeply, slowly. Finally he stepped back. "Let's go home."

In full agreement she nodded, and he draped his arms around her shoulders. "Ready?"

She smiled slowly, and he smiled in return, and she felt as if she glowed with happiness. As they opened the door and walked back through the empty dining room, they found Vicki standing in a corner talking to a man.

"I've been showing Jasmine the house. We just looked at the utility room," Matt said.

Vicki laughed as they walked past, and as soon as they were alone, Jasmine turned to him. "You think that's funny, but you embarrassed me."

"You don't want Vicki to know I kiss you?" he asked with innocence.

"Not in the utility room at this party! It's like we're desperate—"

"No, it's like we're in love," he said, interrupting her.

"How can I argue with that!" she exclaimed, giving up. "Tell the world we've been kissing in the utility room."

"Okay—"

"I'm joking!" she snapped, grasping his arm as he took a determined step forward.

"Let's find Tonia and Russ and say good night," he said, and all through the good-byes and thank-yous, she was more aware of Matt at her side than what she said or did.

The silence of the car enveloped them. Matt pulled her close to him, his hand resting on her knee while they talked about Amarillo, the weather, and her work with his family chronicles, until finally the lights swept over the ranch house, and Wolf bounded out to greet them.

They spent a few minutes petting him, then went inside. Matt locked the door.

He turned to take her into his arms. "You were beautiful tonight. My family loves you."

"That's good. They're nice. I like them."

"Reach into my pocket."

She looked at him quizzically. "You have more than one."

"The right front pocket of my jacket."

"Mmm," she teased, stroking his hip as her hand slid inside. He watched her face as she touched the box.

Ten

She withdrew the small dark blue box, and varied expressions flitted across her features. First surprise, then curiosity, then a dawning realization.

His heart beat like rain in a storm as he watched her open it. Her lips parted, and her breath sucked in in a raspy intake of air. When she looked at him, he saw joy and love revealed unmistakably in her eyes before he caught her as she threw her arms around him to kiss him soundly.

"Will you marry me?" he asked. The words came easily now.

She pulled away, and her eyes sparkled with bright tears.

"Hey, honey, tears?"

"I'm happy. You don't feel suffocated or hemmed in?"

"Never. I feel lost without you," he said gruffly, taking the ring from her hand and slipping it on her finger. It caught the light, but the brightness of the diamond was nothing like the joy shimmering in her eyes, and he felt something warm and joyous filling him.

"I know what I want," he said in a husky voice.

The box fell from her fingers as she hugged him again. The ring and the future were temporarily unimportant while his long fingers moved through her hair, sending pins flying.

"If you'll wait, I'll take my hair down."

"I can't wait," he said, his blood pounding as he watched her. "This is the way the dress is meant to be worn. With your hair down."

The coming separation seemed only a cloud on a far horizon at the moment. Matt's hands and lips and body were the only reality, and she accepted his proposal, his ring, and his kisses without a qualm.

Her lips parted and her dark lashes fluttered down, feathery above her rosy cheeks. Matt felt as if he would burst with need for her. He crushed her to him, kissing her hungrily while he found her zipper and carefully pulled it down. He peeled away the silk, leaning back to look at her.

She was beautiful. The lacy underthings she wore were red, her skin pale, still retaining the tan where she had been exposed to the sun in Patagonia. As he watched her, he pulled off his coat and dropped it on a kitchen chair. "I'll never get enough of you," he said hoarsely, his adoring gaze devouring her.

She drew a deep breath that made her breasts swell against the lace, and he felt as if his senses had been seared. He wanted her to feel the same as he did. He wanted to hear her cry his name, to have her want him. He unbuttoned his shirt, pulling it off.

She moaned softly and stepped close, her slender fingers tugging at his belt.

With his blood thundering in his veins, he picked her up and carried her to the living room, lowering her feet to the floor as he pulled her against him, feeling her full, soft breasts crushed to his hard chest.

"Jasmine, I love you," he whispered. He kissed her and all words were lost.

The next morning she called her parents to tell them the news, and when she heard her mother's voice come on the line, she said excitedly, "Mom, I'm engaged to Matt."

"Oh, Jasmine, sweetie, that's wonderful! I'm so happy for you because I know you love him."

"I do. I really do," she said, smiling up at Matt and squeezing his hand. He kissed her throat, and she closed her eyes.

"Let me get Dad so you can tell him. When will you be home next?"

"I don't know. I'll write. I'll be home soon. Maybe two weekends from now."

"Jasmine, when's the wedding?"

"We decided on the last weekend in May."

"Here's your father."

While she listened to mumbled conversation on the other end of the line, she turned to kiss Matt lightly. She winked at him, and he smiled, moving away from her to get two cups of coffee.

"Jasmine?"

"Dad, we're engaged. Matt and I plan to get married."

"That's fantastic news! We're so glad. He seems like a fine fellow."

"He is a fine fellow," she said with laughter and happiness in her voice.

Her dad laughed. "I take it you're happy."

"Here, you can talk to him." Jasmine thrust the phone at Matt and he accepted it.

"Sir, I love Jasmine very much."

Jasmine moved away, listening to Matt's part of the conversation while she stroked his arm. Finally he handed the phone back, and she talked with her parents a few moments longer before she hung up and turned into Matt's waiting arms.

"You sounded nuts talking to your dad. Fine fellow! Holy smoke!"

"You're my fellow, and such a delectable one at that!" She nipped at his throat, and he swung her around and kissed her.

When he released her, he said, "Now we get to tell my family. They won't take it so calmly. My sisters have wanted me to get married for years."

"Thank goodness they didn't succeed a long time ago!"

"Yeah," he said gruffly. "I called them and asked them to dinner tonight."

"So soon?" she said, wondering if groceries needed to be bought, then remembering Matt's well-stocked pantry.

"Honey, we couldn't keep them away with a cannon. They'll be ecstatic. You're their hope—only little do they know, you're not going to reform me. We won't tell them until you're in the family."

They both laughed, and then he leaned his head closer. His hand drifted over her shoulder and down across her breast, making her tremble with longing.

"Did you know it's been two whole minutes since I last kissed you?"

"I thought it had been an hour."

He didn't laugh as he bent his head lower.

That night, he made the announcement after dessert, and Jasmine saw why he had waited until they were through eating. His sisters whooped and congratulated them. First Tonia hugged her, then Marina. Drake got up and came around to kiss Jasmine's cheek while all the sisters talked at once. "See, my welcome wasn't so damned premature."

She laughed and caught Matt glancing at them, before she turned to find Vicki standing beside her.

"I'm so happy for you both, so very, very glad. I think you'll be good for him."

"I hope so," Jasmine said, realizing Vicki's friendship and approval were important to her. Vicki hugged her briefly, but it made Jasmine feel accepted. Next Russ gave her a quick hug, and as she turned away, she saw Vicki hugging Matt tightly.

They all went into the family room. The sisters couldn't wait to hear about the wedding plans. Jasmine sat on the floor with her legs crossed, and Matt dropped down beside her and pulled her close against her shoulder. As they talked, she felt his fingers turning a lock of her hair. His slightest touch made her breathless, and she couldn't wait for them to be alone, suspecting he felt the same way.

The family left about nine o'clock, and the moment the door closed behind them, Matt pulled Jasmine into his arms. "I knew they loved you when you first came. My sisters aren't dumb."

"They're nice, and I want them to be part of the wedding," she said, and then conversation about the wedding ended.

Monday morning came too swiftly. Jasmine sat up in Matt's big bed, watching as he packed a duffel bag, taking very little with him. He was dressed in khaki pants and a khaki shirt with the sleeves rolled up. His boots were neatly placed by the door, and she knew he had moved around barefoot to keep from waking her. He crossed the room to unlock the drawer below the glass gun cases, and he took out a short, ugly weapon. He stood up with it and glanced at her.

"You're awake."

"Yes. What's that?"

"A pistol. It's an Uzi."

Jasmine felt a cold knot in the pit of her stomach, but she smiled at him, and he put down the Uzi and came over to sit down beside her on the bed.

"I have to go. I'm supposed to leave here by seven."

She nodded, feeling her throat close.

"Oh, Lordy, I love you!" he said, wrapping her in his embrace, and for a moment forgetting time. Her hands slid across the stiff, thick khaki shirt that smelled like new cotton. His muscles beneath the material were hard, very familiar to her now, and very important.

She slipped out of bed and into her robe to go

downstairs with him, knowing they would be alone. It was an hour before Leah would appear.

"What about breakfast?"

"I've already had toast."

She realized how tense he was because his answers to her questions were clipped. She watched as he picked up a holster, and a scabbard with a long, deadly looking knife. He flung them into the duffel bag, and she was forced to face the cold, stark reality that had seemed so far away until now. His jaw was set, and he looked hard and capable of whatever task he had before him, but he was only a man and a civilian, and as vulnerable to bullets, knives, and danger as others. She felt as if her insides were being twisted into a tight knot. It was impossible to talk.

She knew the last thing he would want to see would be tears. She moved away from him, going to get a drink of water. Her hands trembled, and she couldn't drink a drop, but distracted her from having to watch him get ready to go. And then he came into the kitchen and stopped to face her. The pistol was tucked under his arm, the duffel bag was in his hand, and a jacket was slung over his shoulder. "Come tell me good-bye."

She flew to him and he dropped the bag. He shifted the gun so he could hold her with one arm, while he kissed her until some of her terror receded. And then he was gone.

She watched him drive toward the ranch's small airstrip. With Wolf at her side, she waited until she heard the plane's engine and saw the bright blue and white aircraft lift easily off the ground, circling once over the house. She walked down the drive to wave to Matt, and he dipped a wing of the plane. Then it banked, gained altitude, and headed east. She felt as if her heart and soul were being torn out and taken with him. And she hurt more than she would have guessed possible.

With a whine Wolf pawed at her, and she knelt down to hug him, tears making the world watery. "Why do you have a master who has to save the world?" she whispered. Wolf's tail thumped on the dusty drive. She gave his head a scratch and stood up, peering into the empty sky, praying Matt would come home safely.

The first two days were bearable because she knew he couldn't be out of the country and into danger that soon, but on the third morning she discovered work was impossible. Worry was constant, nagging and insistent. Vicki called and asked Jasmine to meet her in Amarillo for dinner and a show, and told her she could spend the night at her apartment in town.

Jasmine agreed, and met Tonia the next day for lunch. The next day Marina came to the ranch and brought Matthew and Lisa. She talked about her childhood, her babies, and Drake's job as vice-president at Rome Aerospace. Jasmine knew all the sisters were making an effort to see to it that she wasn't lonely. But nothing could make up for Matt's absence. And her worries grew each day. The sisters couldn't be there every day, and after the first week, she didn't see them as often. Spring weather made the loneliness more intense, because the nights were warm and inviting. The moonlight and flowers in the yard, the fresh smell of spring hovering over the ranch, made her ache for Matt to be enjoying it with her.

Vicki came out Sunday afternoon, and while

they ate chicken sandwiches in the kitchen, she asked, "Are you all right out here alone?"

"I'm fine."

"Would you rather go back to Houston or come stay at my place until he gets back?"

Losing what little appetite she had, Jasmine shook her head. "No, but thanks for the invitation. I'm finally getting a lot of work done on the letters and journals. And it doesn't matter where I am. Nothing can stop my worries about his safety."

Vicki looked down swiftly. "I know." She raised her blue eyes. "I guess we hoped you'd issue an ultimatum to him."

"I don't think your brother is one for ultimatums."

"I suppose not. I think that's what happened before in his life." She ran her hand across her temple. "We worry so much about him. I do."

She was silent, and Jasmine knew she was making an effort to control her emotions; Jasmine had to do the same for Vicki's sake.

"He hasn't given any indication of refusing to go on those missions?"

"No. Just the opposite. He seems determined to go."

"He's had several close calls," Vicki said in a soft voice, and it was all Jasmine could do to hold back tears.

There was a long silence, and finally Vicki shook her long, dark hair away from her face and brushed invisible lint off her black sweater. "I'm not doing you a bit of good. Let's watch something on television or go look at the journals you're reading."

"The journals it is!" Jasmine said, her voice conveying a brightness she didn't feel. "They're more interesting." They sat and read for two hours, pointing out special letters to each other, and Jasmine felt better until Vicki left.

For a long time Jasmine stood in the doorway listening to the silence around her, looking at the stars that seemed as remote as Matt. Of all the men on earth to lose her heart to—why did she have to pick one who gave home and family such low priority?

She found no answer in the empty night. Wolf scratched at her leg with his paw. "Come on inside. At least you don't wander." She let Wolf into the house. She knew he would be a better watch-dog out on the grounds, but she was lonesome.

Each day was a tormenting solitude the likes of which Jasmine had never known. Loneliness and fear for Matt's safety became relentless companions. And as the days passed, her fear grew in alarming proportions, because she didn't hear a word from him. She had to keep a clamp on her imagination. She could too easily conjure up the desert and a thousand possible dangerous situations for Matt. She tried to sound bright and chipper when she talked to her parents on the phone.

She knew it was ridiculous to hope Matt would contact her, but she longed for his voice, just to know he was alive. She took his picture out of her billfold and put it on the table beside the bed. She spent long periods of time staring at it, wondering about him, what drove him to leave home and place himself in absolute danger.

And slowly, as she faced a future filled with months at a time away from him, worrying while he was in danger, she began to realize she couldn't live that way. She stared at her diamond engagement ring for minutes on end, feeling an invisible tie to him, even while he was so far away. Torn with agony, she knew she loved Matt beyond belief. She always would. But she couldn't stand being separated from him for weeks while she wondered if he had been captured or shot down over hostile land.

One night, dressed in her blue cotton robe, she sat on the edge of the bed and turned the ring around and around on her finger. Tears spilled over her cheeks. She couldn't accept his way of life, and she didn't want to try to change him or plead with him. Feeling forlorn, she removed the ring and placed it on the table. Then she flung herself down on the bed and cried, knowing no one would hear her sobs or know how badly she hurt.

From then on she moved woodenly around the house, and with each passing day her fear increased. She had time to think clearly and carefully, to make her decisions without Matt's distracting influence. And she began to reach some definite conclusions. He had always insisted he needed his freedom, but what they had was too fine and special to give up without a struggle. She would make an effort to get him to see both sides, to see what he would lose, too, because she knew their love was lasting and true.

The next weekend she flew home and spent two days driving her car back to the ranch so she would be able to drive home if she had to.

Late one night, two and a half weeks later, she sat in her robe and nightgown with the windows open, the May breezes bringing sweet, fresh air into the room. For the past two hours she had been trying to read letters, and as she made notes, Wolf's head jerked up. She watched him, aware of her isolation. She couldn't hear a sound, and felt a prickle of fear. His long ears twitched, and he looked as if he were listening. Then his tail began to thump. He jumped up and ran to the back door, and then she heard a motor. Only certain cars could bring that reaction from the dog—the ranch vehicles that he knew.

Her heart thudded, and she shoved aside the papers to follow Wolf to the back door. As lights flooded the drive, she watched the familiar Jeep slide to a stop. For a moment relief outweighed every other emotion. Jasmine leaned against the wall, saying a silent prayer of gratitude that Matt was home. Feelings of joy, relief, and love overpowered her, but they were tempered now by the knowledge that she couldn't live this way for years to come. And she would have to tell him. She prayed he cared and loved her enough to listen to reason.

He stepped out of the car and she stared at him in shock. His beard was thick and tawny, his hair was longer and tangled, his khakis were ripped and dirty and stained with blood, and his upper arm was bandaged.

Tears streamed unheeded down her cheeks as she ran to him. He caught her with his good arm, crushing her tightly to him.

"Matt!" she cried, hugging him, running her hands over him, catching the smell of smoke and sweat in his clothing.

"Don't cry," he said hoarsely.

She stood on tiptoe, and pulled his head down.

He kissed her roughly, his mouth crushing hers as his tongue thrust deeply, taking her sweetness with an uncontrolled hunger. "I can't pick you up," he said gruffly.

She hurried inside with him, and he kicked the door shut as he caught the belt of her robe and yanked it free.

He shoved away her robe, his hands grasping the neck of the gown and yanking it down, oblivious to the popping buttons or his wounded arm.

"Matt, wait . . ."

"I can't." He hugged her to him, his hard arousal thrusting against her. Her fingers unfastened his belt and tugged down the zipper. Moments later, when he pulled her down onto the oval rug on the kitchen floor, all her resolve vanished.

Hours later, she lay in his arms in his big bed while he slept. She brushed her fingers lightly on his cheek and across his beard. Tomorrow morning, she would talk to him, try to get him to take a close look at their future, try with all her power to make him stop and see what they stood to lose.

It was nearly dawn before she fell asleep and when she woke up, Matt was beside her, his hand tangled in her hair. "I can't look at you or touch you enough," he said in a husky, velvet voice that wrapped her in warmth.

He pushed away the sheet, his eyes caressing her before he came down to kiss her. Her arms went around his neck. In a moment, he turned his head slightly. "I have to go back next Friday, at the end of this week. And I'll probably be gone a while, but I'll be back in time for the wedding."

Her eyes flew open and she twisted away to gaze at him. "You can't go again—you're hurt!"

"It's a cut, nothing serious, and it'll heal."

"Do you usually go back so soon?"

"No. Something came up this time."

"Matt, I have to ta—"

His kiss stopped her words, and conversation was lost as he pushed her down on the pillow.

Two hours later she had bathed and dressed. She wore her pink cotton shirt and jeans. Her hair was loose, and it swung lightly back and forth with each step as she went downstairs to find Matt.

He had given Leah the day off, and from the smell of coffee and bacon drifting up through the house, Jasmine knew he was cooking breakfast. She moved woodenly, knowing what she had to do, afraid a part of herself would be destroyed if he didn't yield.

She found him putting fluffy, scrambled eggs, thick slices of ham, and hot biscuits on the table. A tall glass of chocolate milk waited for her, but she'd lost her appetite weeks ago.

He had a clean bandage on his arm and wore a gray sweat shirt with the sleeves pushed high, his tight, faded jeans, and his familiar brown boots. The beard was gone, and he looked like himself, sexy and too appealing.

"Doesn't that hurt your arm?"

"Not really. Come eat."

"You sit down while I pour the coffee."

"Hurry up, because I'm famished. I haven't had food like this since I left home."

She took a bite and politely chewed it, but it

was like a lump of clay in her mouth. She tried to wash it down with some chocolate milk.

"What happened while I was gone?"

"You tell me first. How did you get hurt?"

He gave her a quick look. She saw the shuttered expression on his face and knew he wouldn't talk about his mission. "I just cut my arm. Tell me about the ranch."

"Nothing unusual happened," she said, watching him eat with gusto. "Your sisters have entertained me royally." She realized he had lost a few pounds; his body was all lean, hard muscle. "I had lunch innumerable times with them. I've stayed with them, and they've been out to the ranch to visit."

"Did they bother you?"

"Heavens, no! I have three-fourths of your letters organized."

"Miss Efficiency."

Jasmine found it difficult to smile.

He stopped eating and lowered his fork to his plate, his brows coming together in a frown. "What's wrong?"

"You're very perceptive. Eat your breakfast, and then I want to talk to you."

Eleven

He stared at her for a full minute, then tossed his napkin on the table and leaned back in his chair. "Let's talk now. What's wrong?"

"You're supposed to leave again right away?"

"That's right," he said abruptly.

"While you were gone, I had a lot of time to myself to think. And a lot of time to worry about you." Each word was hard to say, but she looked him in the eye as she said, "I was terrified for your safety."

"I'm careful," he said gruffly, his blue eyes darkening.

"I know you're the man I will love all the rest of my life."

His features softened, and he reached across the table to take her hand. "Come here and sit on my lap." She did, resting her arm on his shoulder as he pulled her head down to kiss her. She put her heart and soul into the kiss, as if she could

162

sear him and forge a binding link that would hold them together.

She felt his fingers at the buttons of her shirt and caught his hand, looking at him solemnly. "Matt, I can't live this way, and you don't have to. What we have is fine and good and can be lasting."

"What are you trying to say?" he asked gruffly.

"I can't live with the worry."

Something flickered in his eyes, and his jaw hardened. She felt a sense of panic because she suspected she was going to lose him.

"I have to have my freedom, my space," he said brusquely.

She watched him, aware he did have space—the ranch with its vast expanses of empty prairie, the land unbroken as far as the eye could see. He had had his solitary rides until she came along. He had the *Paradise* and a whole lonely ocean of space. In her heart she didn't feel she crowded him. The only change, the only demand was to give up the life-threatening missions.

"You have space, and you have freedom, but this is above and beyond that. It isn't duty—you've done enough for your country now."

"I have to do this, Jasmine," he said, and this time his voice was cold and harsh and so unlike him.

"Do you get paid?"

His gaze became glacial. "Yes, a lot."

"Is the money that important?"

"I'd do it for free. You should know I don't have to earn money this way if I don't want to. Between the ranch and the plant, I can do as I please."

"If it's guilt over Teddy, you've paid your price and you shouldn't have felt guilty in the first place!"

She rose and moved to the sink, watching him stand and face her, his hand resting on the counter beside her.

"I don't feel guilty about my brother," he said firmly. "I thought you were different. I thought you would accept me and my life as I am, not try to make me over into what you want!"

The words stung like blows, but she lifted her chin. "I adore you, and that's why I'm fighting for our love. Otherwise I would have packed and gone the first week after you left."

"I won't give up my freedom," he said, astounded at the change in her. "I've been tied down for years. I want to go when I want, do what I want. I explained how I feel." Disappointment uncurled and consumed him, blinding him to everything else. She was the same, no different from other women he had known, no different from his sisters. They all wanted to hold him.

"I'm not asking you to give anything up."

"The hell you aren't!"

"The missions aren't necessary. You can have all the solitude and freedom you want, but we can't build a marriage around separation, secrecy, and danger."

He felt a tight knot of anger as he stared at her. She gazed at him steadfastly in return. "How long do you intend to continue to volunteer for these missions?"

"As long as I feel like I can benefit people," he said evenly. Her eyes shimmered with tears that she tried to blink back, and he felt a twisting ache in his heart. He could see the effort she was making to keep control of her emotions, and he tried to hold the same tight rein on his anger and pain.

"We never talked about children, but I want a baby. What kind of father would you be? Off in a jungle, your life in danger—because you volunteered for it! If you had to, it would be different. But to go deliberately is a world of difference!"

"It's something I feel strongly about, something I have to do."

"Forever?"

"Of course not, but I don't want to give it up now. I'm not ready to," he snapped, thinking he wasn't ready because he was beginning to feel as if she were trying to fetter him with invisible chains. "I know what I want, and this is part of my life."

"Maybe this time," she said in a tense voice, "*you're* the one looking at the shell instead of what's inside, Matt."

"What are you talking about?" he said, scowling at her.

"I'm not arguing just for me, but for us." She made a fist and pressed it against her heart. "We have something wonderful and special. *We fit, Matt.* Don't just look at that shell you've developed through the years, but look inside at your heart."

Her words startled him, but he was too angry to heed them. "I know my heart—I love you, but I love the woman I knew—you're different. You changed fast when a ring was on your finger!" he said, and she blinked as if he had struck her. "I'm leaving Friday morning!" he added bitterly.

"Then I'll be gone before you are," she said.

He was angry and hurt, and he wanted her badly. Suddenly, he reached out to pull her roughly into his arms, ignoring the shooting pain it caused in his arm. He crushed her to him, kissing her until he felt the stiffness go out of her, until he felt her response. He continued passionately, making her return his kiss, realizing when abandon had overtaken her anger. He made love to her, silently, fiercely, yet not roughly. He didn't have to be rough to get a full response from her, to stir her body to eagerness, to a wanton passion.

Ignoring the pain it caused, he picked her up and carried her to a bed where he discarded his clothes rapidly, peeling off hers without regard to her few feeble protests which he kissed away swiftly.

As he was poised above her with her hips raising to meet him, he stopped. "You want to give up what we have when we make love?"

"Matt!"

"Do you, dammit?"

"No, I don't! That's why I want you to take a long look inside your heart." Suddenly she twisted and wiggled away, moving out from under him. She had taken him by surprise and he watched her, her wide green eyes and her bare breasts that bore faint marks from his mouth.

"I love you, Matt," she whispered. "I want our love to grow and expand and last." She kissed him, her lips on his flat stomach. "Let me show you how I love you," she said in a low voice, as her hands drifted over him. Then she turned, her dark hair tumbling over her shoulders as she began to kiss and stroke him. Suddenly, he groaned and rolled her over, raising himself above her to possess her. She clung to him, crying out in ecstasy, and he heard his own voice calling her name.

They sank down onto the bed, breathing hard.

Their bodies were damp with perspiration, and they both lay quiet until he moved away, picking up his clothes and leaving the room. She gathered her things, and left the room to shower and dress. She was defeated. He had shown his determination in his lovemaking, and she knew what she had to do. It hurt with blinding, agonizing pain. Numb, she stared at herself in the mirror. Her lips were flushed from Matt's kisses, her cheeks rosy. She decided to wait until Friday morning before he left. If he hadn't changed his mind, she would pack and go.

Downstairs she found him cleaning up the kitchen. He glanced at her as she crossed the room and held out the ring. "When are you leaving?" he asked flatly.

"When do you want me to go?"

"I don't," he said. His tone was impassive, and she wondered if he hurt half as badly as she did.

"I'll stay until Friday morning."

He leaned down to kiss her tenderly, and it hurt to have him be kind and gentle and at the same time as unyielding as granite.

"Your arm's bleeding again. Let me change the bandage."

"Too much lovemaking," he said lightly, but his familiar grin didn't surface. She changed the bandage and as she worked, he continued talking, "I was on the trail and suddenly we were jumped. One man was shot. I got this wound from a knife."

Her fingers shook as she thought about the terrible danger he had been in and his seemingly casual attitude about it, and she knew she had made the only decision possible.

• • •

Friday morning, she came downstairs to find Matt in the kitchen. Leah was gone, and she was sure he had given her more time off so they could be alone. He was dressed in khakis and boots, and she guessed he was going to leave within the hour.

She was packed and ready to leave herself, and without a word she turned and went back to her room to get her things. Matt was standing in the hall when she came out. "You're going?"

"Aren't you?"

"Yes, I am. It's part of my life, and it's a part I don't want to change. I guess I wasn't meant to be domesticated." His cheeks were red, and his voice was tight and raspy, as if he were having difficulty controlling his emotions. "I warned you I couldn't make a lasting commitment."

"And you feel suffocated by what I want you to do?"

"You've given me a stifling ultimatum," he said sharply.

"I asked you before to take a good look at your heart, Matt," she responded firmly. "Look beyond my ultimatum, as you call it. I'm not giving you an order. I'm trying to save our love, and if I can't do that, I have to survive. It's an instinct."

Anger flashed in his expression again. She was independent, and he knew she wouldn't change her mind. And he couldn't change his life just because it didn't suit her. He took the suitcase from her hand and put it in her car. When he turned around, Jasmine was standing behind him. "Have you told my sisters?"

"I told Vicki. She'll tell the others."

"What a blow to them," he said bitterly, his thoughts on Jasmine. He wanted to crush her to him. He wanted the woman he had left behind when he had flown away almost a month ago. "I don't go often. Usually about twice a year. These two trips coming so close together are unusual."

She shook her head, and he could have sworn he saw tears fill her eyes, but she blinked them back swiftly. "I have to leave. We're at an impasse."

He couldn't keep from reaching for her, but he forced himself to merely hold her shoulders, not haul her into his arms as he wanted to do with all his being. He hurt badly. "Dammit, I can't help the way I am!"

"You're not cast in an unchangeable mold," she said. Her words had a hollow ring to them. "I think you're still looking at that shell. I don't think you've ever stopped to look at your heart."

He cursed, but she didn't care. Instead, she held out her hand. "Here."

He looked down and accepted the shell he had given her on board the *Paradise.*

"That is what I am now, Matt. An empty shell. You have my heart."

"Oh, dammit, Jasmine—!"

She climbed into the car, and he slammed the door behind her. He leaned down to kiss her through the open window, forcing his tongue into her mouth in one last passionate kiss. Then she started the motor, put the car in gear, and drove away.

He hurt in a way that he hadn't hurt before. He was amazed at how badly he felt. He had broken up with women in the past, and had tried to console several who had taken the breakup very hard. "Getting your own back, old buddy," he told himself, kicking a rock angrily with his toe. He had to leave too, but he stood in the warm sunshine staring at the plume of dust from Jasmine's car that gradually faded out of sight. He held out his palm and looked at the empty shell, and her words seemed to float around him like leaves scattered on a pond.

. . . you have my heart. . . . We fit, Matt. Don't just look at that shell you've developed. . . . Look inside at your heart.

Flinging the shell away with all his might, he swore sharply. It sailed in an arc and landed beyond the fence in the field. Turning away, he strode inside to get his things and get out of the empty house. He went quickly to the hangar, and once airborne was unable to keep from flying low over the highway and looking at the cars below. He spotted her car easily and wondered if it would occur to her that he was overhead. He lifted his gaze, clamped his jaw closed until it ached, and flew over the car without looking back.

Jasmine tried to drive and see through tears at the same time. Nothing in her twenty-eight years had caused her so much pain. And she suspected that in all her life, she would never again hurt as badly.

She heard the drone of the plane, after it had passed over, and she saw that it was Matt's. And then it was gone. Forever. It seemed so final.

She parked on the side of the road to cry until the tears wouldn't come anymore.

It was a long drive to Houston from the ranch and she got in late that night. She was exhausted, numb, and suffering an enduring, steady pain. She decided she would call her parents the next day, when she was more composed. She dreaded the call, because she knew how much they wanted her to be happy. And they liked Matt. She lay awake in bed that night, worrying about him, wondering where he was at the moment. And she wondered if she would ever be able to forget enough so that she wouldn't always feel like someone was turning a knife in her heart.

The next day she didn't call her parents and she didn't give a thought to job hunting. She had enough money from the job at the ranch to enable her to wait several months before she had to get another job. By the time she started to phone her parents on Sunday, she remembered they had planned to go fishing at Caddo Lake for the weekend. The pain was all-consuming. She couldn't eat, she couldn't sleep. As she lay in bed Sunday night, worrying about Matt and where he was, she sat up and turned on the light to get his picture and look at it.

She was filled with longing and the need to see him. She swung her feet to the floor and held the picture in her hand, staring at his smiling image, which was captured forever on the bit of paper. His arm was around her, and suddenly, she wondered if she had really looked at her own heart.

She didn't want them to go their separate ways, to let Matt lead a life without her. As bad and as painful as it had been to wait for him, to spend the long, lonely hours in choking fear that he might be hurt, she had been part of his life and he had been part of hers.

She knew what she wanted to do, what was in

her heart. She threw back the covers, her hands shaking in her haste. "Please, let him be all right," she prayed, wishing she could talk to him, if only for a few minutes.

She was going back to him. Any small part of his life was better than nothing at all. She was an empty shell without him. And while empty shells were pretty, they weren't very functional.

He had said he wouldn't be back for three weeks. Three empty weeks at the ranch. As she flung her suitcase on the bed, she remembered when she had been on board the *Paradise*. Matt had said, "I come here when I want to unwind. . . ."

The *Paradise*! He would go to the *Paradise* when he got back. She was certain. And if she stayed on the *Paradise*, she could be away from family and friends until she worked things out with Matt. She would be only an hour's drive from her apartment if she wanted to come back to town.

She glanced at the clock and knew it was late to call Leah, but she was compelled to do whatever she could to get closer to Matt. When she heard Leah's familiar voice, she gripped the phone tightly.

"Leah, this is Miss Kirby. I'm sorry if I woke you."

"That's all right. How are you, Miss Kirby?"

"I'm fine. I wish you'd give Mr. Rome a message for me when he gets home."

"Yes, ma'am."

"Will you tell him I'm staying on the *Paradise*?"

"Yes, ma'am." Leah's voice seemed to brighten. "We miss you here."

"Thank you, Leah. I hope I'll be back soon."

"Yes, ma'am. That would be nice! That would be real nice! Miss Kirby . . ." She paused for a long moment and then said hesitantly, "I've been here a long time, and I've never seen Mr. Rome as happy as he was when you were here. I'll see he gets the message."

"Thanks, Leah. Thanks so much!"

Jasmine replaced the receiver and smiled, feeling as if the world had been lifted off her shoulders. Talking to Leah had been a tie to Matt, a reassurance. She stood up and worked swiftly, planning to go to the *Paradise* the next morning. She would wait to phone her parents until she had talked with Matt and knew exactly what the future held.

And now all she had to do was wait and pray that he was safe. She prayed that their differences wouldn't affect his concentration when he was in danger.

She was too edgy to sleep, and early the next morning she drove to Galveston, bought groceries, and boarded the *Paradise*. The day was clear, a blue sky with sweeping banks of white clouds, and white breakers rolling steadily onto the sand. She drove to the southwest side of the island, parked the car, and walked along the beach, staring south, knowing that Matt was somewhere hundreds of miles away.

"Please be careful," she whispered. "Come home to me." An image of his powerful body with its myriad scars came to mind. She knew now how he had gotten the scars, and she could finally accept, to a degree, the life that lay ahead with him. The prospect of life without him was ghastly and too bleak to contemplate.

She had worn a comfortable old denim skirt that was full and pleated with tiny buttons down the front. She also wore her pink shirt. The wind coming across the Gulf was brisk and cool, but she was comfortable. She walked up the beach to the dunes, and sat down on a log to stare out to sea, trying to gain some sense of closeness to Matt. The same sky was over him, the same sun. The dainty golden bracelet on her arm reflected the sunshine. He had given her that bracelet on the Saturday that seemed so long ago now. She closed her eyes tightly again to pray for his safety.

An hour passed while she sat quietly waiting, knowing she would spend hour upon hour waiting for him if she married him. And she could accept it now, because she had learned that the alternative was impossible. With a sigh she stood up. Jamming her hands into her pockets, she strolled down to the water's edge.

Meandering along the hard-packed gray sand, she listened to the breakers roll in, as gulls circled overhead, spreading their wings and sweeping gracefully out over the water. Wind tangled her black hair while whitecaps appeared and receded in a steady rhythm.

A long shell caught her eye. It was embedded in the wet sand, and she pulled it free, washing it in the next surge of water. Its lines were blue, the ridges faintly pink. It was lovely, and she smiled and dropped it into her pocket. She was a long way from the car, and she turned around to start back.

In the distance she saw a man walking toward her along the beach, and suddenly, she became alert to her surroundings and her situation. She had wandered far from her car. It was Monday morning on an empty, isolated beach, and she was alone and vulnerable. She had been so busy concentrating on Matt, she hadn't given a thought to where she was or what she was doing. Her pulse jumped a little in fright. She thought about cutting across the dunes toward the highway, but it might be as deserted as the beach.

Then, to her enormous relief, she saw a car drive down to the beach and park. A man and woman with fishing gear climbed out. She quickened her step, wanting to get to her car while someone was still around. The couple could easily get back in their car and go.

The man still approached her in a long, lazy stride. He was closer now, and her heart turned over because he resembled Matt. Her pulse settled right back to normal. Every tall, blond, broad-shouldered man she'd seen during the past few days had brought a skip to her heartbeat.

The couple turned along the beach in the opposite direction, and Jasmine began to jog, wanting to get nearer to them as quickly as possible. Her gaze swept back and her pulse took another lurch. The man did resemble Matt. He had the same tangled blond hair and the same wide, powerful shoulders. She couldn't keep from staring at him, imagining and wishing . . .

Her breath caught, and she stopped in her tracks. It *was* Matt!

Twelve

She blinked and stared. He couldn't be here on the beach. He wouldn't know where to find her. No one but Leah knew she was here. He was supposed to be in some distant land, not Galveston!

Then he was only yards away. She ran to him and he caught her up in his arms. They kissed wildly, and she held him as tightly as possible, as he let her slide slowly down the length of his body until her feet touched the sand. She was crying at the same time she kissed him. Her hands tangled in his hair, then ran across his shoulders as if she were making certain he was truly there. Finally she pulled back to look at him. "Why? How come you're here?"

His dancing blue eyes told her more quickly than his words that he loved her. Totally. She trembled as she stroked his cheek. "I thought long and hard about everything you said. And I couldn't stand to be away from you, or know that when I returned you wouldn't be waiting—always."

"Oh, Matt!" She had to kiss him again, to affirm all she felt. This time when she pulled away slightly, she asked him, "How did you get out of going back?"

"I just asked them if they could get someone else to take my place. They said yes, so that was all there was to it. I told them I'm retiring."

Her eyes brimmed with tears. "You did that for me?" she asked. She suspected it hadn't been as simple as he made it sound, but she didn't care. The important thing was—he wasn't going back on dangerous missions.

He leaned closer, his gaze engulfing her. "I did it for us—what you told me to do. We do fit, Jasmine. I realized what I was throwing away. Life wtihout you would be unbearably emp—"

She flung herself against him, kissing him, stopping his words because they were no longer necessary. This time he was the one who leaned away and broke off their kiss. "Let's go back to paradise," he said huskily.

She smiled and wiped her eyes. "The *Paradise*, you mean!"

"I know what I said." They walked together, clinging to each other, his arm around her shoulders, hers around his waist.

"How in the world did you find me?"

"Deductions, a hunch, luck. You weren't on the boat. I asked around the docks, and someone saw you turn left out of the parking lot. See, that's the advantage of inquiring about a beautiful woman—someone will have noticed her."

She laughed. "Go ahead and tell me how you found me."

"My cool, logical mind solved the problem," he

said smugly, his happiness as radiant as sunshine. "If you had been going straight back to Houston, you would have turned right, so I circled around downtown Galveston, looking at all the cars, then I drove down and cruised along the beach, looking for your car. I just kept going. I've been looking for you for about two hours."

She paused to look up at him. "It was impossible to think about life without you," she said quietly, her dark hair swirling across her cheek.

"I can't get enough of you," he answered in a deep voice, pulling her to him to kiss her again. She pressed against the length of his muscular body, feeling she couldn't get close enough or hold him tightly enough, reassuring herself that it wasn't a dream. He was here! And he wasn't going back into danger!

"Ouch! Dammit!" he yelped, moving away and looking down at her. "What the hell—?" He rubbed his thigh and she remembered the shell. She pulled it out of her pocket and laughed.

"I'm sorry! I saw a pretty shell while I was walking."

He grinned. "I forgive you. Once upon a time, I would have accused you of trying to neaten up the beach, but not any longer. C'mon. I want to be alone with you." He glanced around. "Of course, we're alone here . . ."

"No! The lecherous and leering side of your personality is showing! This is a public beach. Control yourself."

"I can't," he said, and his voice was solemn again.

"Let's hurry," she urged, trotting to keep up with him.

"You know you shouldn't have been out here all alone. It isn't safe."

"I realized that when you first appeared and I didn't know it was you, but earlier, I wasn't thinking clearly. I was thinking only about you."

He groaned and his arm tightened around her. "We really are alone . . ."

"No!" she exclaimed, taking his hand and tugging.

It seemed like an eternity until they were below on the *Paradise*. At the foot of the companionway, Matt caught her arm and turned her to face him. "We're really alone now."

She framed his face with her hands. "You're sure you can live with your decision? I don't want you to feel suffocated."

"I felt worse than suffocated thinking about life without you," he said, his voice hoarse with emotion. The tone of his voice tugged at her heart as strongly as what he'd said. While he talked, she slipped her hand beneath his shirt, caressing the warm flesh of his back.

He smiled at her. "I'd made arrangements at work and everywhere else to be away for three weeks. Now I wouldn't cheat you out of the wedding we planned, but why don't we slip down to a justice of the peace and marry as soon as we can?" Her heart began to skip beats as she listened to him. A twinkle appeared in his eyes. "We can marry in church later."

"Two weddings?" she asked teasing him. "That's mighty binding. You won't feel as if someone's double knotting that noose around your neck?"

"Try me. What do you want to wear for your first wedding, Miss Kirby?"

"I bought a long white lace dress while you were gone, but it's being altered in Amarillo. The only skirt I have on the *Paradise*, other than the one I'm wearing, is my pink wool with the matching pink sweater."

"Sounds grand. You're beautiful in your pink wool."

She narrowed her eyes and tilted her head to one side. "What are you going to wear?"

He grinned, and the creases in his cheeks deepened and lines fanned from the corners of his eyes. "I happen to have brought a dark suit along."

"You brought a suit? When did you go back to the ranch?"

"I got back there about an hour after you had talked to Leah. I flew to Houston at dawn this morning."

"And you *planned* on getting married when you came down here!"

"I thought I might persuade you."

They both laughed, and he caught her up in his arms again.

"Oh, Jasmine, you were right, so very right. I used to go into dangerous situations because I needed some kind of release. It gave an exciting edge to my life and made me forget the responsibilities I had at home and my worries about finances," he said. "On assignment I had to live moment by moment, worrying about something that really didn't eat at my heart. And I'll admit, I did feel guilty about letting Teddy go on the trip abroad. And the first few missions I went on helped shut out the pain of losing him. He was my little brother and I loved him." His voice became rough again as he talked. He ran his hand tenderly over her head, stroking her hair. "I have a request."

"What?" she whispered, aching to kiss him.

"If we have a boy, can we name him after Teddy?"

Tears threatened to spill down her cheeks as she stood on tiptoe to kiss him. "Of course."

"We'll have to get a blood test and license. I want to be married and be on our way on the *Paradise* as soon as possible. If your folks can keep a secret, you could call them to come join us."

"Oh, Matt! I'd love to. I couldn't bear to call and tell them I'd given your ring back, so they—"

"Hey! I forgot. Here's the ring."

He slipped it on her finger.

"You did plan this down to the last detail!"

He grinned and held out his hands. "Our ship is ready to sail. The galley's stocked, and you're wasting time talking."

Two days later, she stood at Matt's side as they spoke their vows in front of Justice Henry Barnstetter. She was dressed in her pink sweater and skirt, and Matt was in his dark suit. In her hands she carried a bouquet he had given her of pink carnations, deep pink roses, lily of the valley, baby's breath, and daisies. He wore a white daisy on his lapel.

"I now pronounce you man and wife." Justice Barnstetter turned to Matt. "You may kiss the bride." Matt turned her to face him, lifting the veil her mother had worn at her own wedding thirty-one years earlier.

Jasmine's heart pounded with joy as they walked

out of the white frame house and into the sunshine. They both hugged her parents and kissed them good-bye. "Thanks, Mom. Don't forget—it's a secret. You'll have to watch us do this all over again."

"I'll be glad to!" her mother said, her eyes shining.

Jasmine hugged her dad once more, and waved to them again from the car as they drove away.

Matt pulled her close. "You're a beautiful bride."

She laughed, feeling giddy with happiness. "In my pink sweater and skirt!"

"Particularly in your pink sweater and skirt."

"Hey! Slow down or we'll get a ticket!"

"I'm anxious." He parked near the *Paradise* and scooped her up and carried her on board. As soon as they went below, she pulled off the veil and let it drop to the floor.

He smiled at her. "You're not as neat as you used to be."

"I know what's important in life," she said, kicking off her shoes and letting them drop too.

"I can't call you Miss Efficiency now."

"It's Mrs. Rome—but I'm still efficient. I'll show you how efficient," she whispered, kissing the corner of his mouth. "And thorough," she whispered, brushing a kiss lightly across his lips. "And competent," she said, placing her mouth firmly on his.

His arms crushed her tightly. Jasmine's heart pounded with joy. In Matt's arms, she was *in* paradise as well as on board it!

THE EDITOR'S CORNER

In celebration of our first anniversary we printed the following in our Editor's Corner—"It seems only a breathless moment ago that we launched LOVESWEPT into the crowded sea of romance publishing." Many things have happened in the years since we published the first LOVESWEPTs. The market has seen the birth of new romance lines and, sad to say, the demise of romance lines. Through it all we have remained true to the statement we made in our first anniversary issue—"Each time we've reached the goal of providing a truly fresh, creative love story, we find our goal expands, and we have a new standard of freshness and creativity to strive for." We try. Sometimes we don't hit on the mark. Sometimes we astonish even ourselves by hitting it square in the center. But thanks to the support of each of you, all the LOVESWEPT authors are growing and learning, while doing what we most like and want to do. We have even more of a challenge in presenting not just four, but six terrific romances each month.

It is such a pleasure to have a Helen Mittermeyer love story to kick off our expanded list next month. In **KISMET**, LOVE-SWEPT #210, Helen gives you another of her tempestuous romances with a heroine and hero who match each other in passion and emotional intensity. Tru Hubbard meets Thane Stone at one of the most difficult times in her life—certainly not the time to fall head-over-heels in love. Yet she does, and it looks as if she's rushing headlong into another emotionally disastrous situation, not just for herself, but for Thane, too. And so she runs as far and as fast as she can. But she's failed to realize her man is ready to walk through fire for her. A very exciting love story!

If there's a city more romantic than Paris, someone has failed to let me know. I think you'll love the setting almost as much as the heroine and hero in Kathleen Downes's LOVESWEPT #211, **EVENINGS IN PARIS**. From the moment Bart Callister spies a lovely mystery woman on the deck of the Eiffel Tower until he has pursued and caught lovely Arri Smith there's breathless, mysterious love and romance to charm you. But Arri's afraid. She knows she's no siren! You'll relish the ways that Bart handles her when she thinks *all* her secrets have been revealed. A true delight!

It is a great pleasure for me to introduce you to our new author Margie McDonnell and her poignant romance **BANISH THE DRAGONS**, LOVESWEPT #212. I had the pleasure of working with Margie before I came to Bantam, so I know she writes truly from knowledge of the heart and of courage, traits

(continued)

that she shows in her own life. Here she brings you a captivating couple, David and Angela, who know the worst that life has to offer and whose bravery and optimism and head-over-heels love will make you sing for joy, when you're not cheering them—and the children they deal with in a very special summer camp. A truly heartwarming, memorable debut.

Sit back, relax, and prepare to chuckle with glee and thrill to romance as you read Joan Elliott Pickart's **LEPRECHAUN**, LOVESWEPT #213. Imagine Blake Pemberton's shock when, home sick with the flu, a woman appears at his bedside who is so sprightly and lovely she seems truly to be one of the "little people" of Irish legend. And imagine Nichelle Clay's shock when she shows up to clean an apartment and confronts a sinfully gorgeous hunk wrapped in one thin sheet! A charming romp, first to last.

Welcome back Olivia and Ken Harper with **A KNIGHT TO REMEMBER**, LOVESWEPT #214. Tegan Knight sizzles with surprises for hero Jason Sloane, who is sure the T in her first name stands for Trouble. She'd do just about anything to thwart his business plans, but she hadn't counted on his plans for her! And those she cannot thwart—but what red-blooded woman would even want to? Two devilishly determined charmers make for one great romance.

LOVING JENNY, LOVESWEPT #215, showcases the creativity and talent of Billie Green. There are very few authors who could pull off what Billie does in this incredible story. Her heroine, Jenny Valiant, crashes her ex-husband's wedding reception to inform him their quickie divorce was as valid as a three dollar bill. Then she whisks him away (along with his bride) to sunny Mexico for another, but this time valid divorce, and sweeps them all into one of the most tender, touching, humorous romances of all time. A fabulous love story.

Enjoy!

Carolyn Nichols

Carolyn Nichols
   Editor

LOVESWEPT
Bantam Books, Inc.
666 Fifth Avenue
New York, NY 10103

Imagine yourself Loveswept®